THE UPRIGHT REVOLUTION

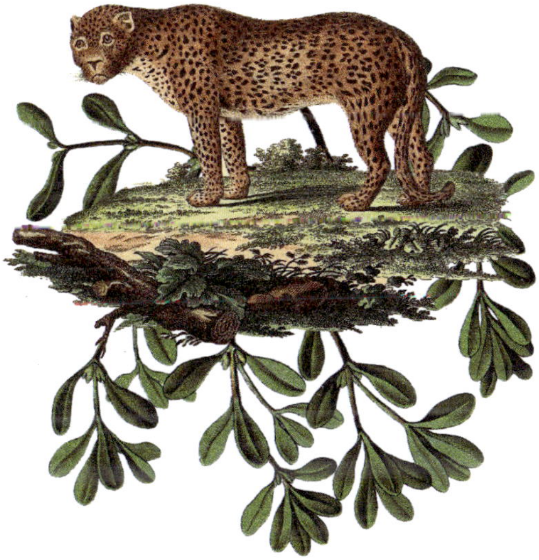

THE AFRICA LIST

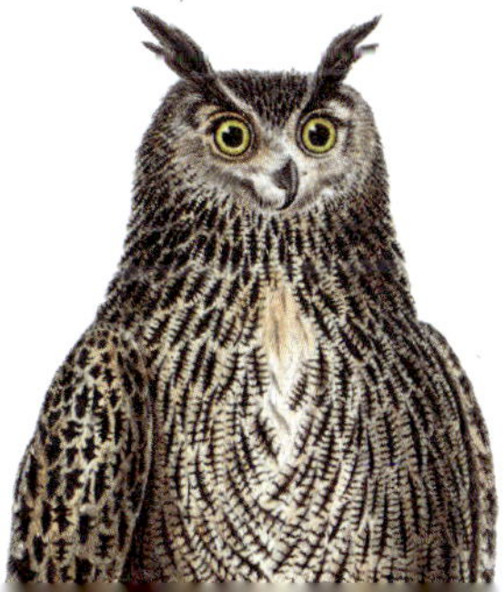

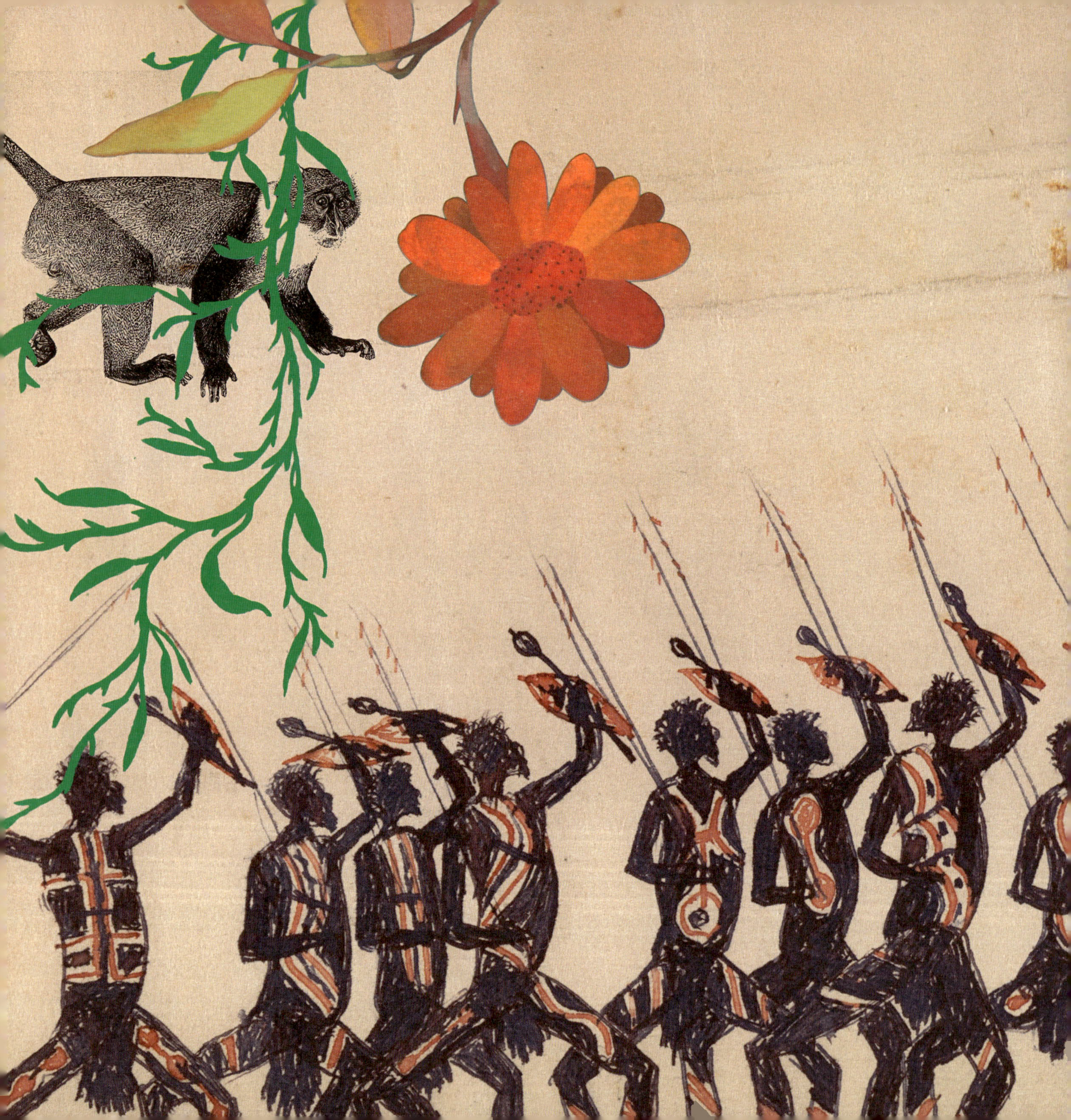

Ngũgĩ wa Thiong'o

THE UPRIGHT REVOLUTION

OR WHY HUMANS WALK UPRIGHT

ILLUSTRATED BY SUNANDINI BANERJEE

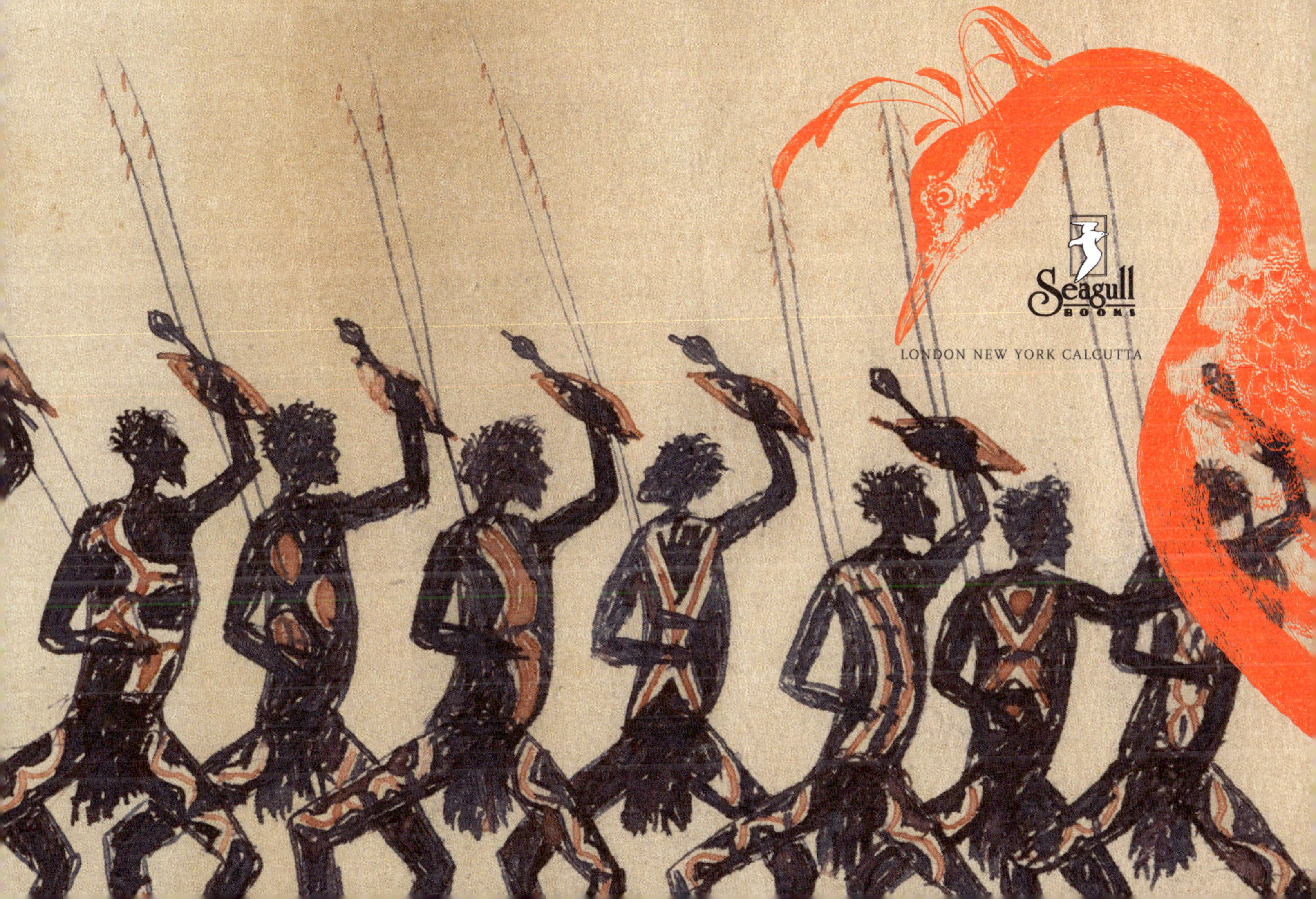

Seagull Books
LONDON NEW YORK CALCUTTA

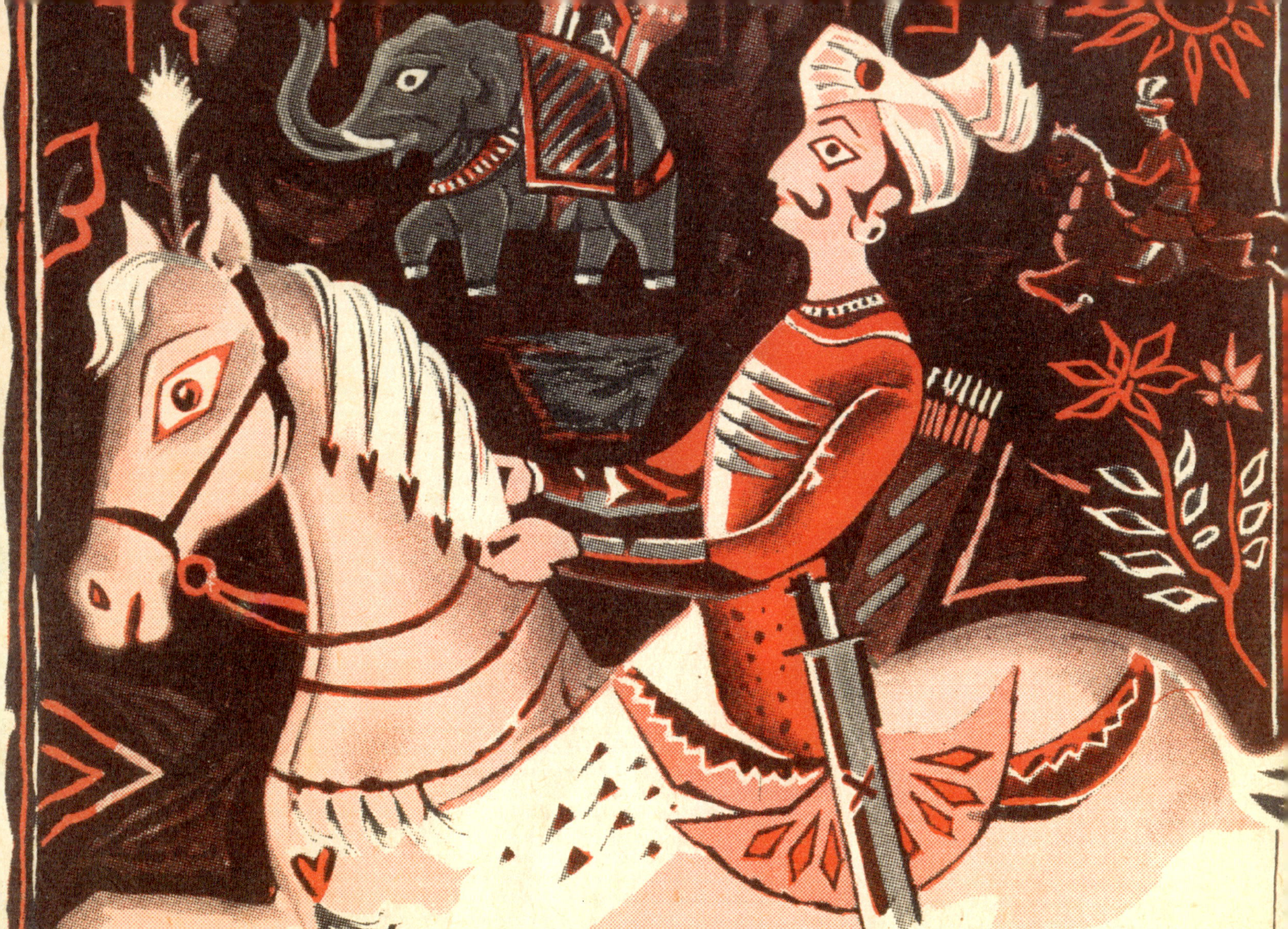

Seagull Books, 2019

Translated from the original Gikuyu by the author.

ISBN 978 0 8574 2 647 5

British Library Cataloguing-in-Publication Data

A catalogue record for this book is available from the British Library

Designed by Sunandini Banerjee, Seagull Books, Calcutta, India

Printed and bound by Hyam Enterprises, Calcutta, India

THE UPRIGHT REVOLUTION

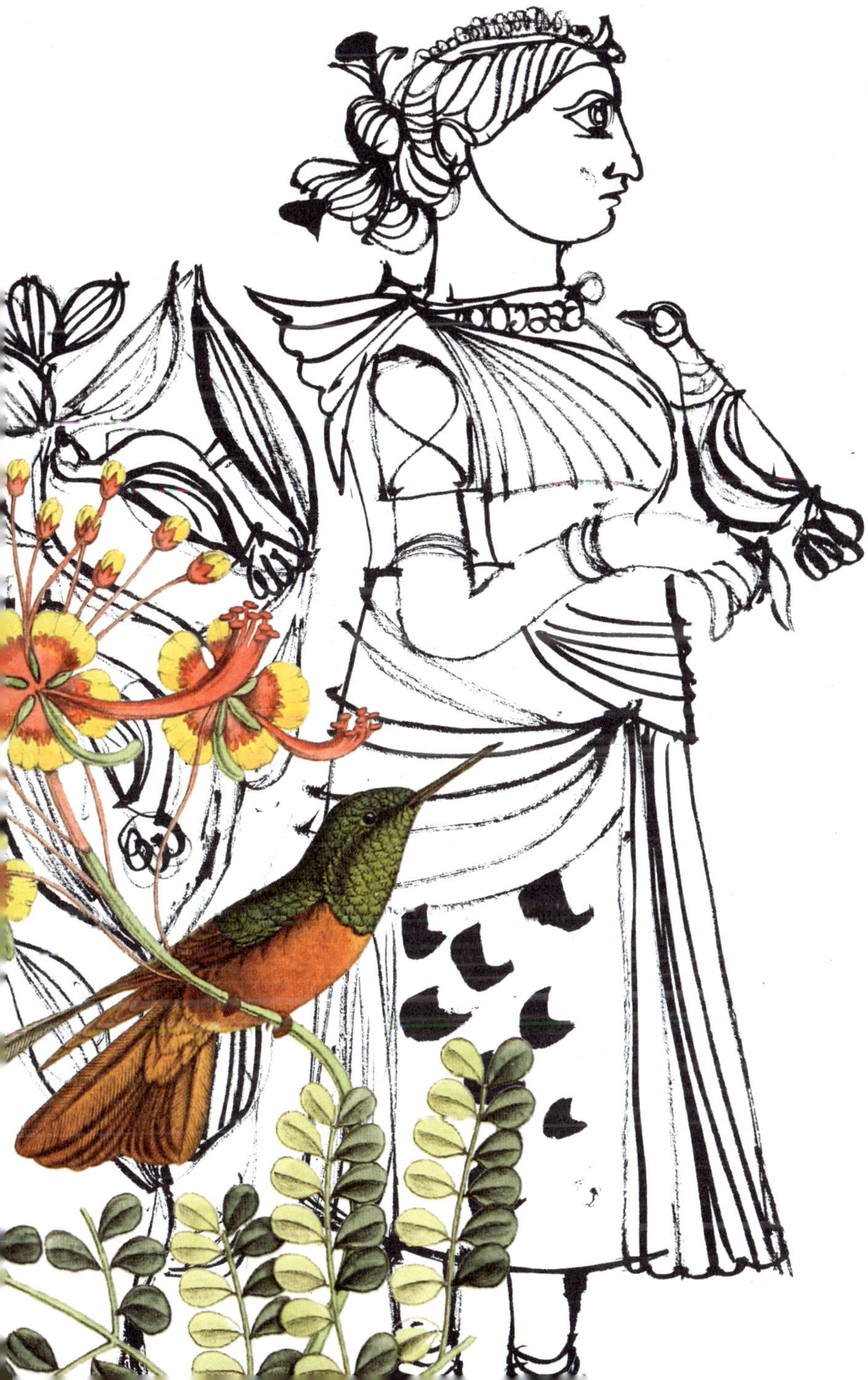

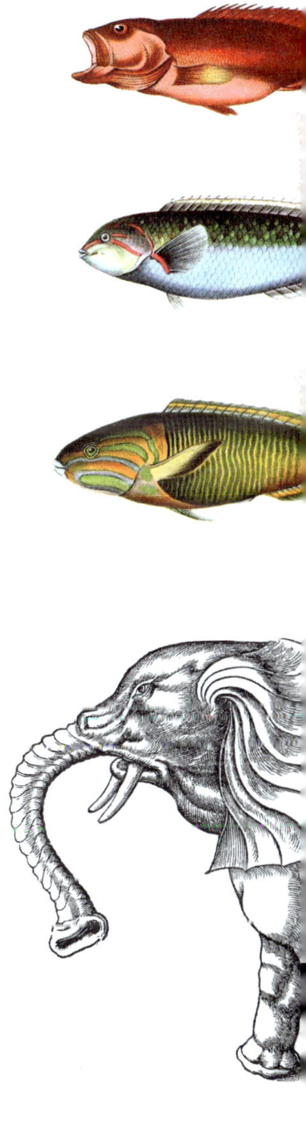

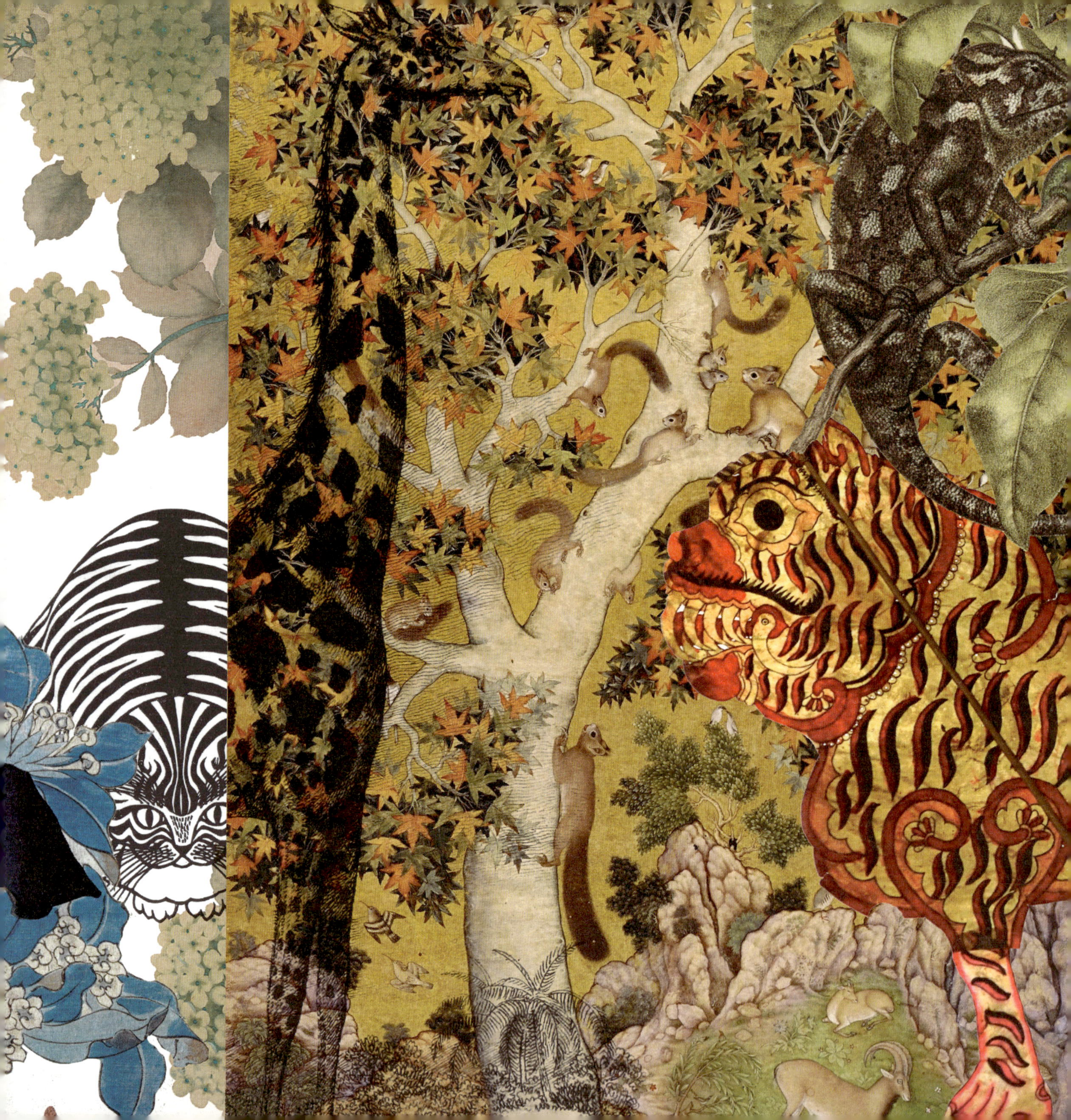

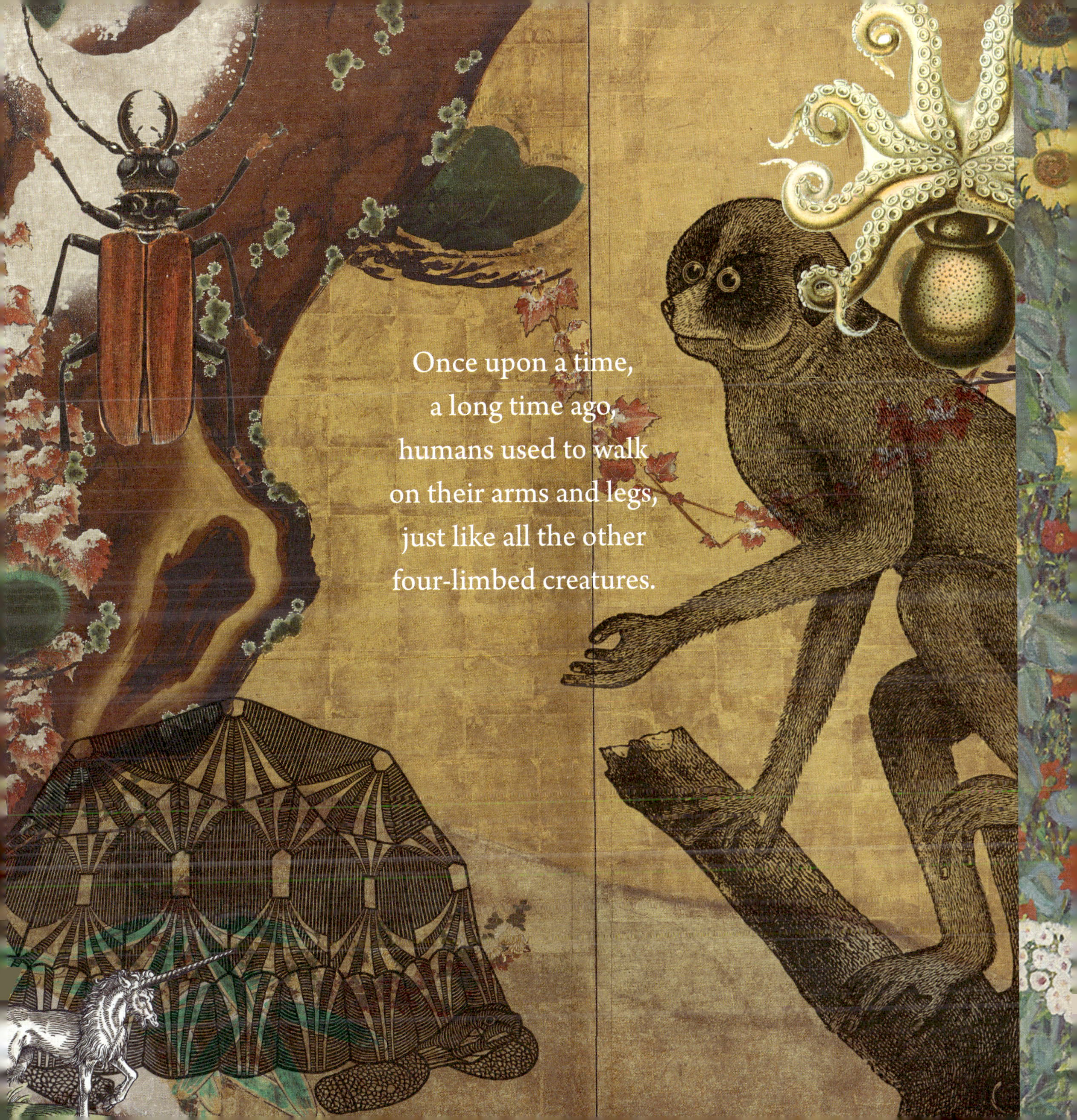

Once upon a time,
a long time ago,
humans used to walk
on their arms and legs,
just like all the other
four-limbed creatures.

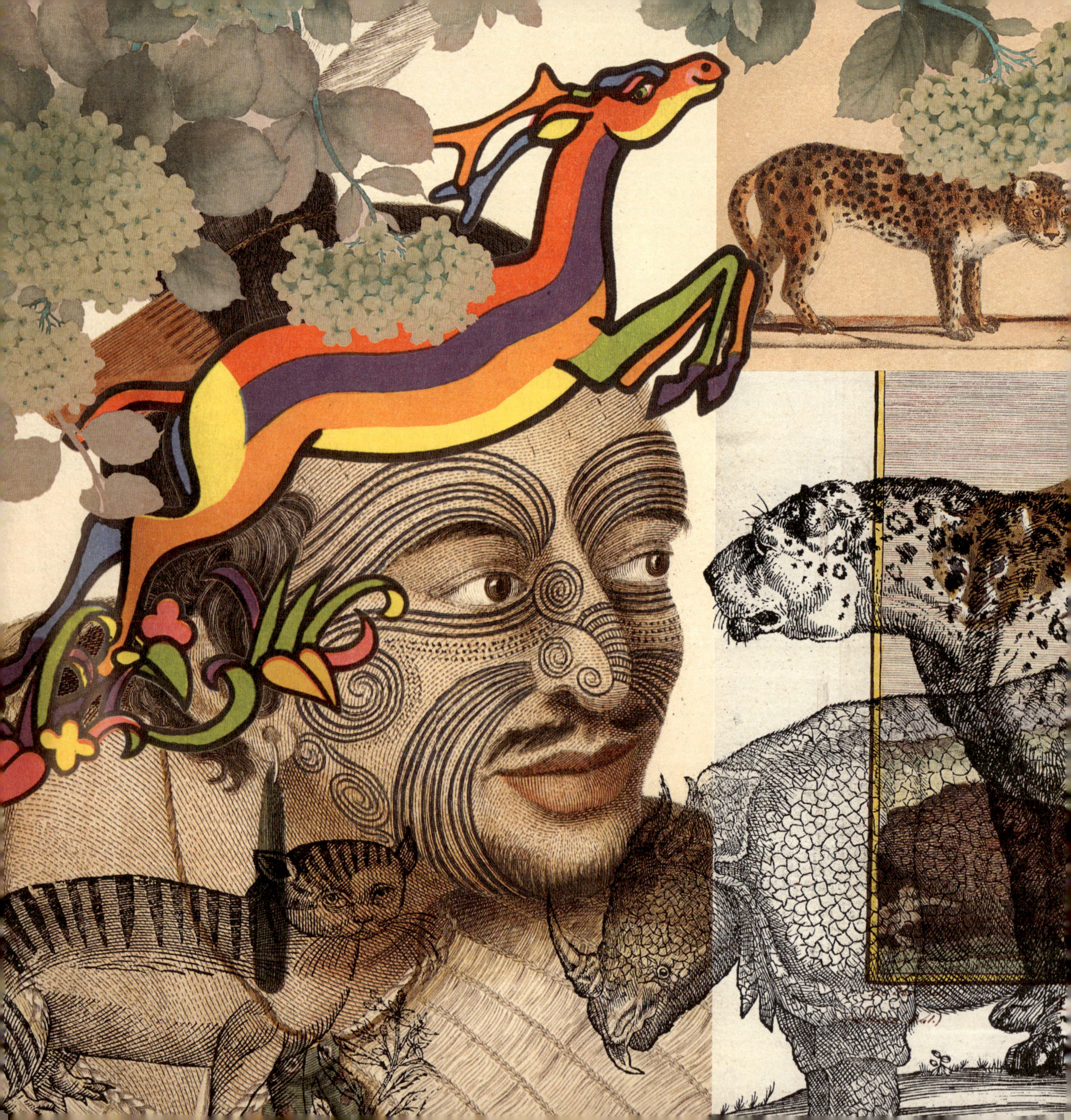

Humans were faster
than hares,
leopards or rhinos.

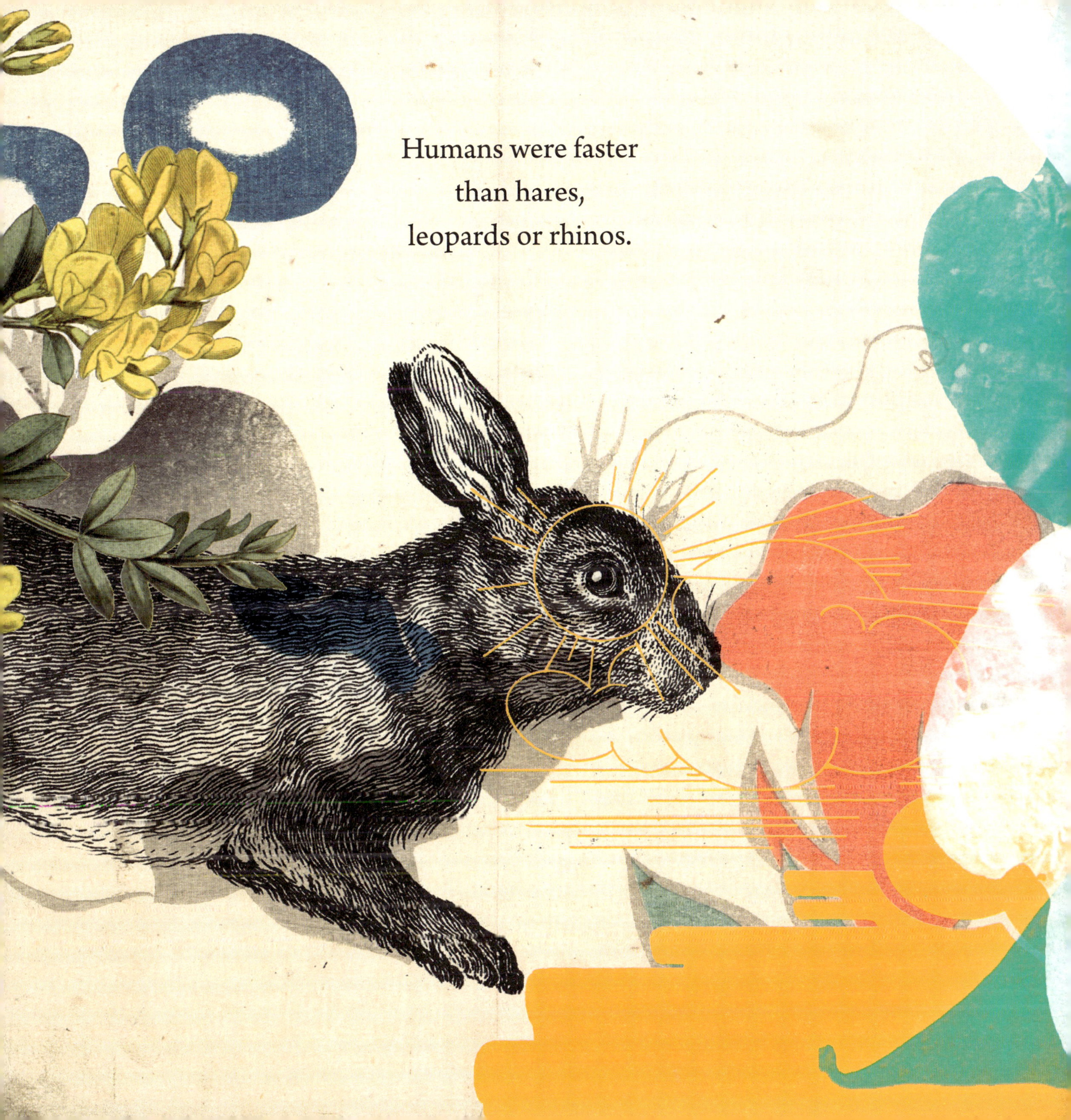

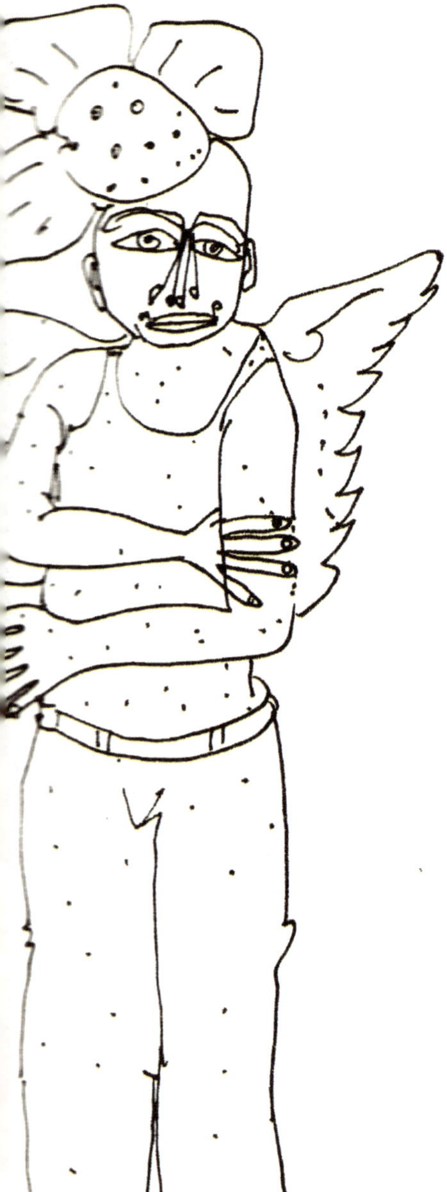

Legs and arms were closer than the other organs, and had similar joints: shoulders and hips; elbows and knees; ankles and wrists; feet and hands, each ending with five toes and fingers.

Hands and feet had similar arrangements—five toes and fingers, from the big toe and thumb to the smallest toes and pinkies. In those days, the thumb was close to the other fingers, the same as the big toe.

The legs and arms thought of each other as cousins. They helped each other carry the body wherever it wanted to go—to the market, the shops, up and down trees and mountains, anywhere that called for movement.

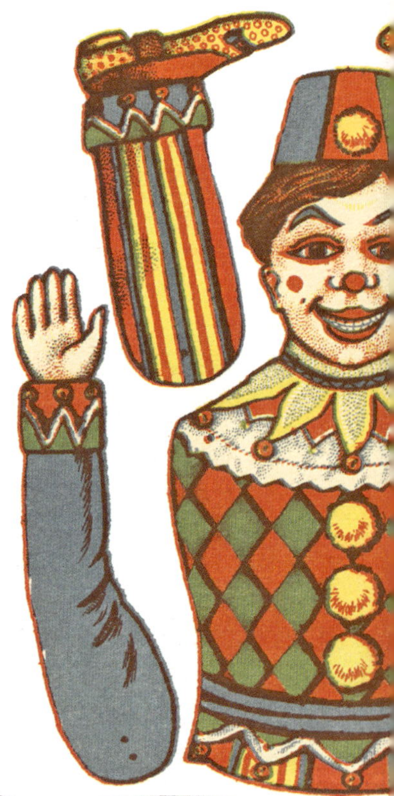

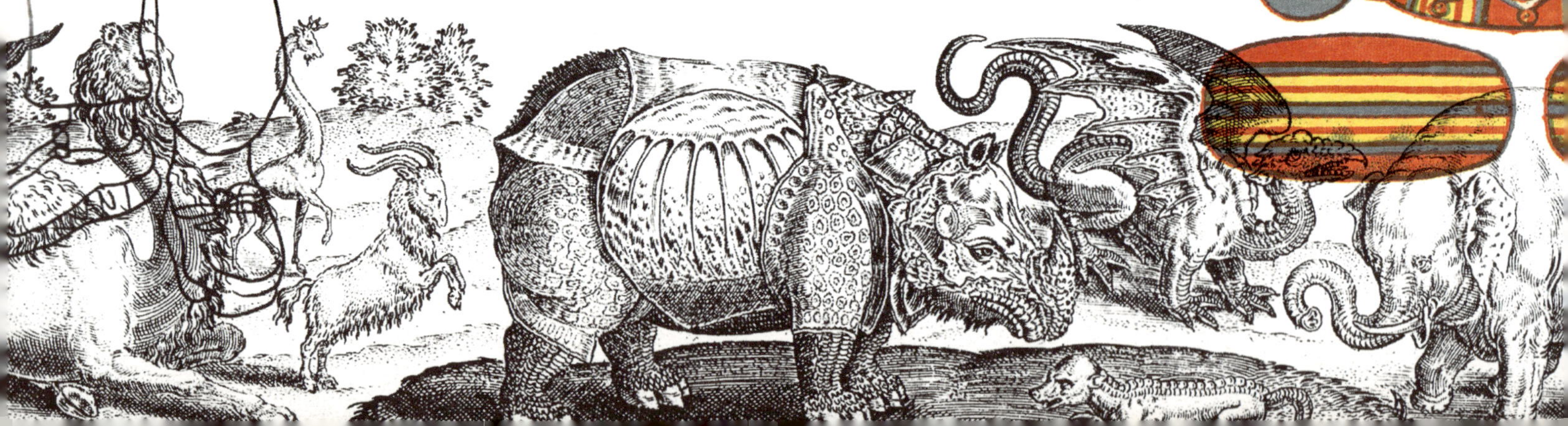

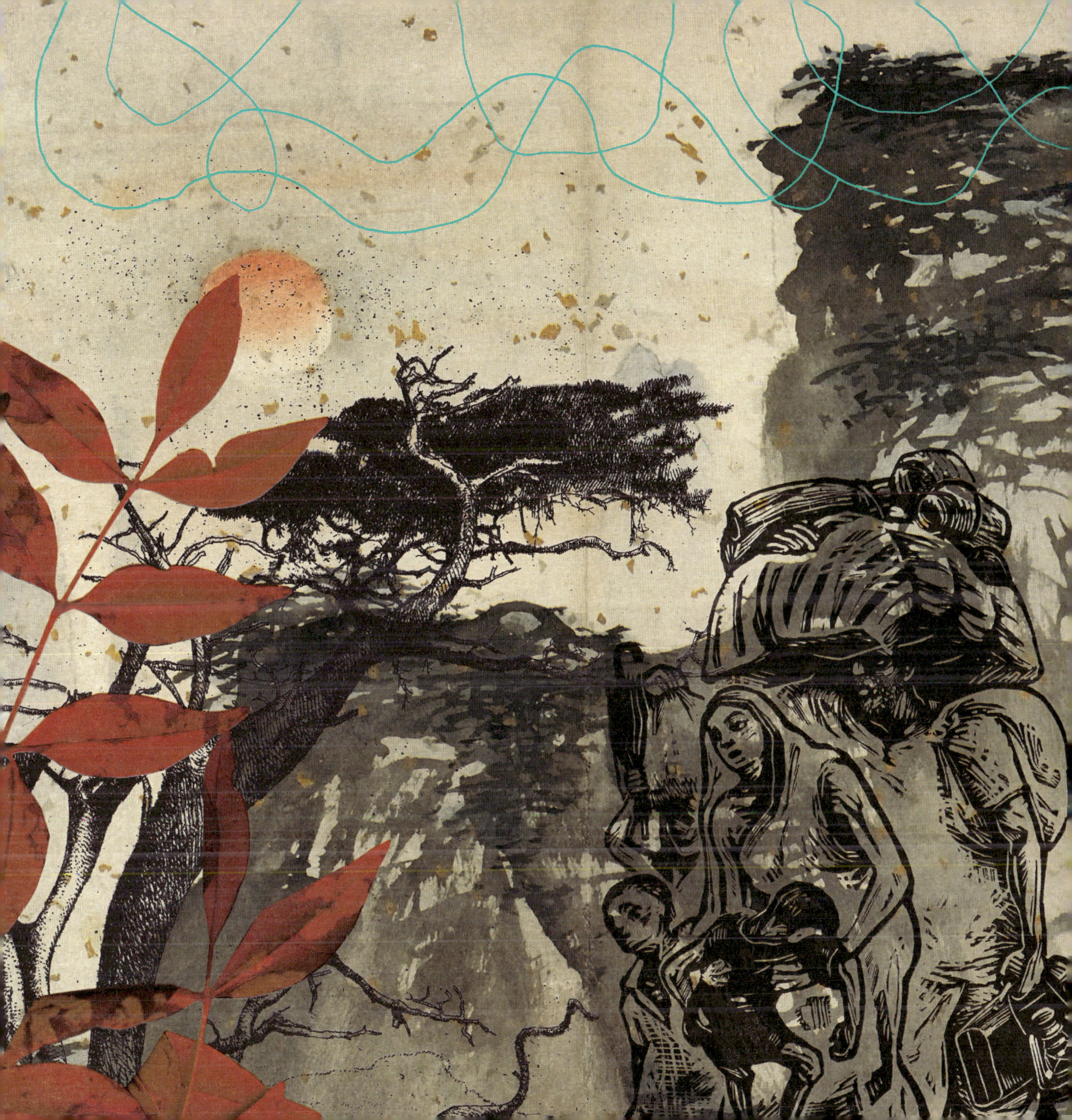

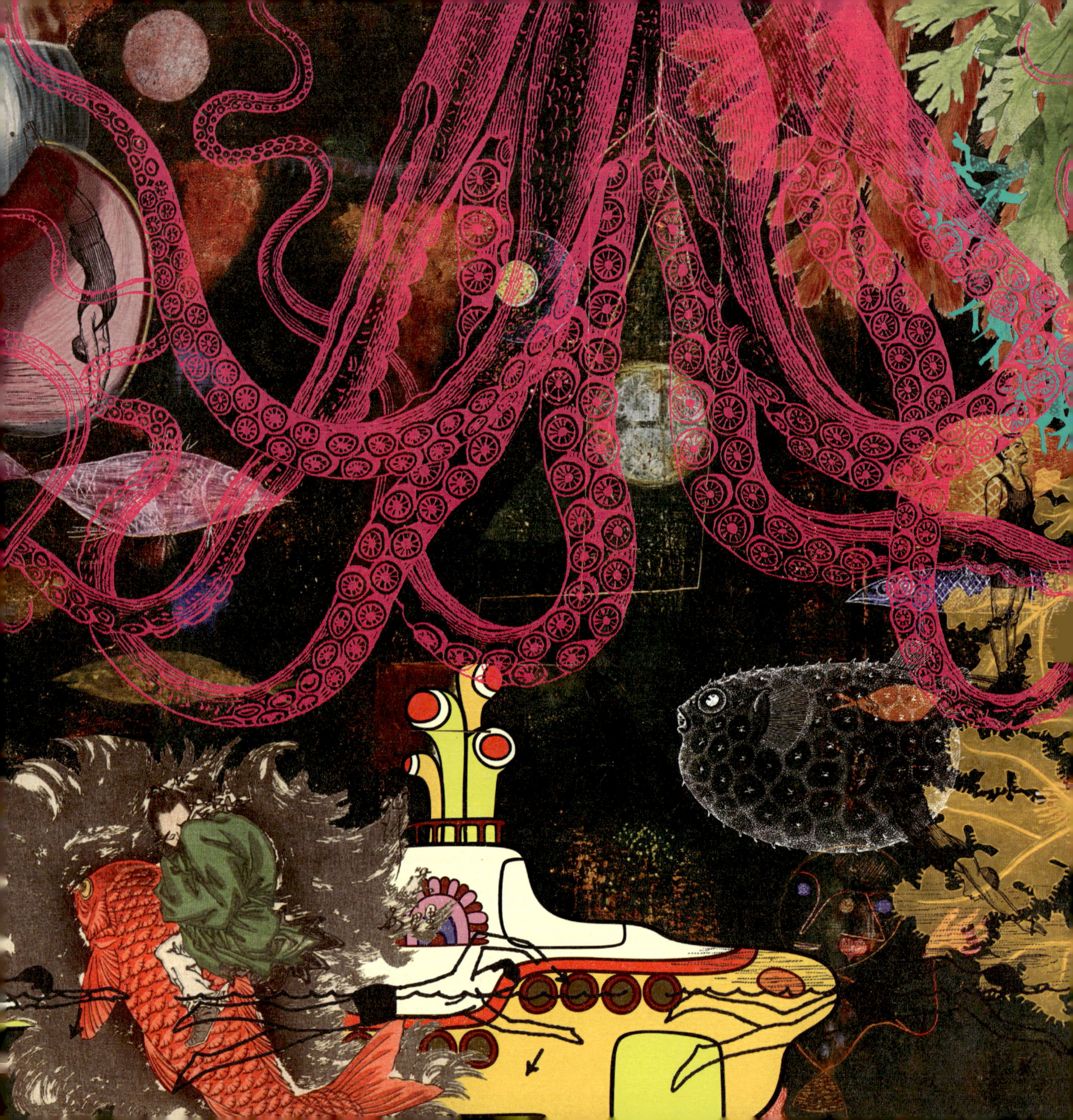

Even in the water, they worked well together and helped the body stay afloat or swim or dive.

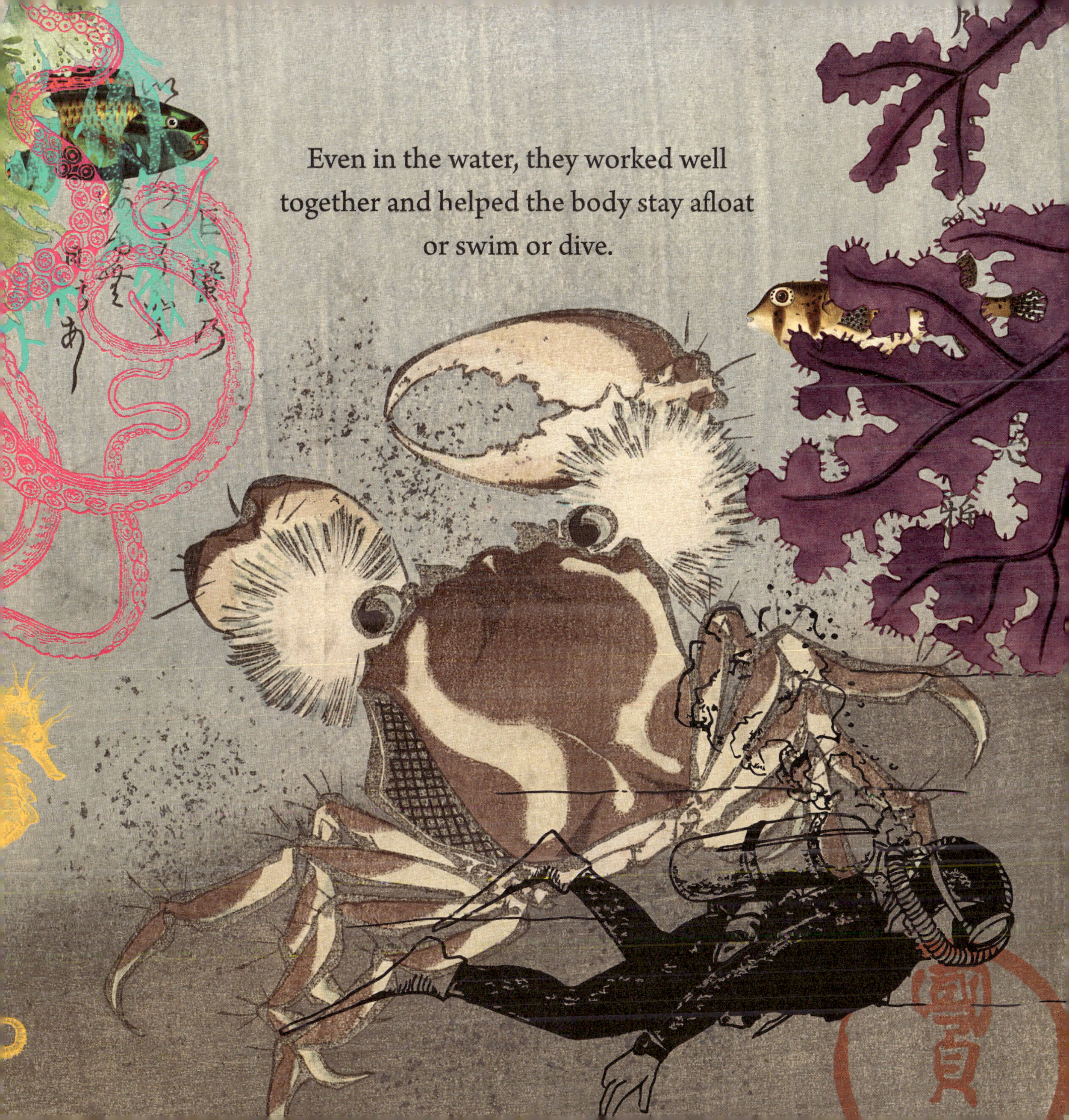

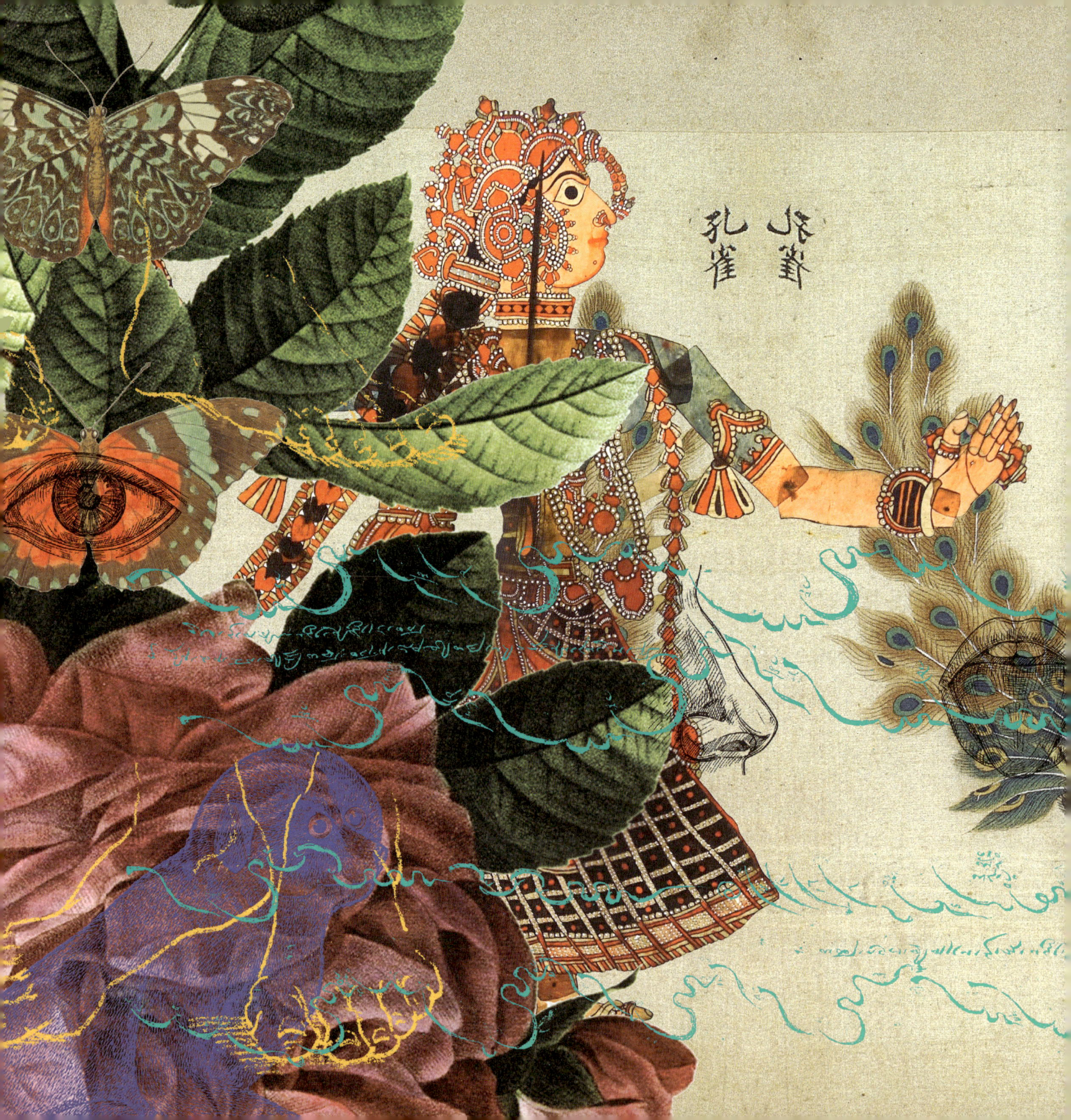
孔雀
孔雀

Democratic and egalitarian in their relationship, they could also borrow the uses of the other organs—sounds from the mouth, hearing from the ear, smell from the nose and sight from the eyes.

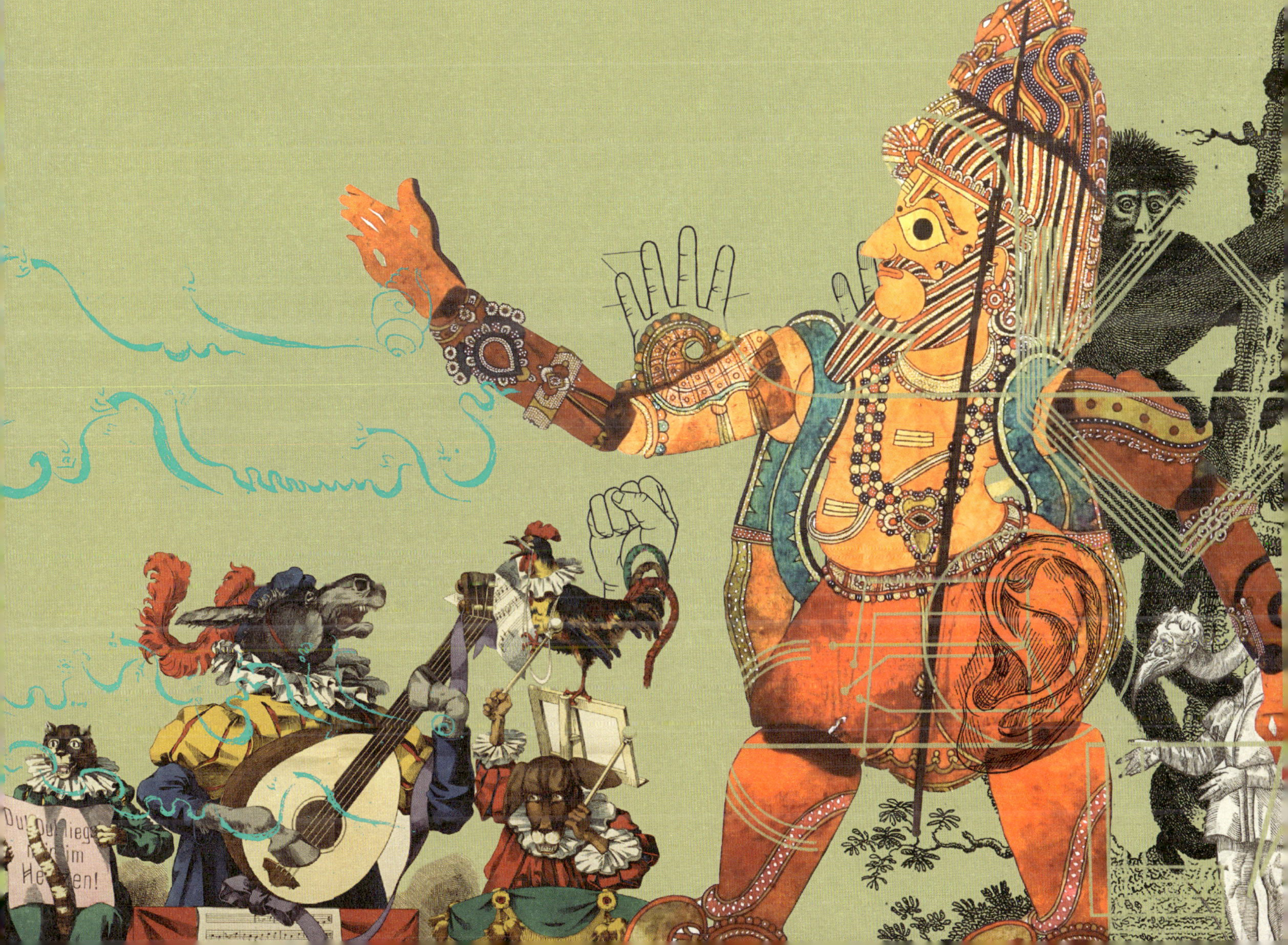

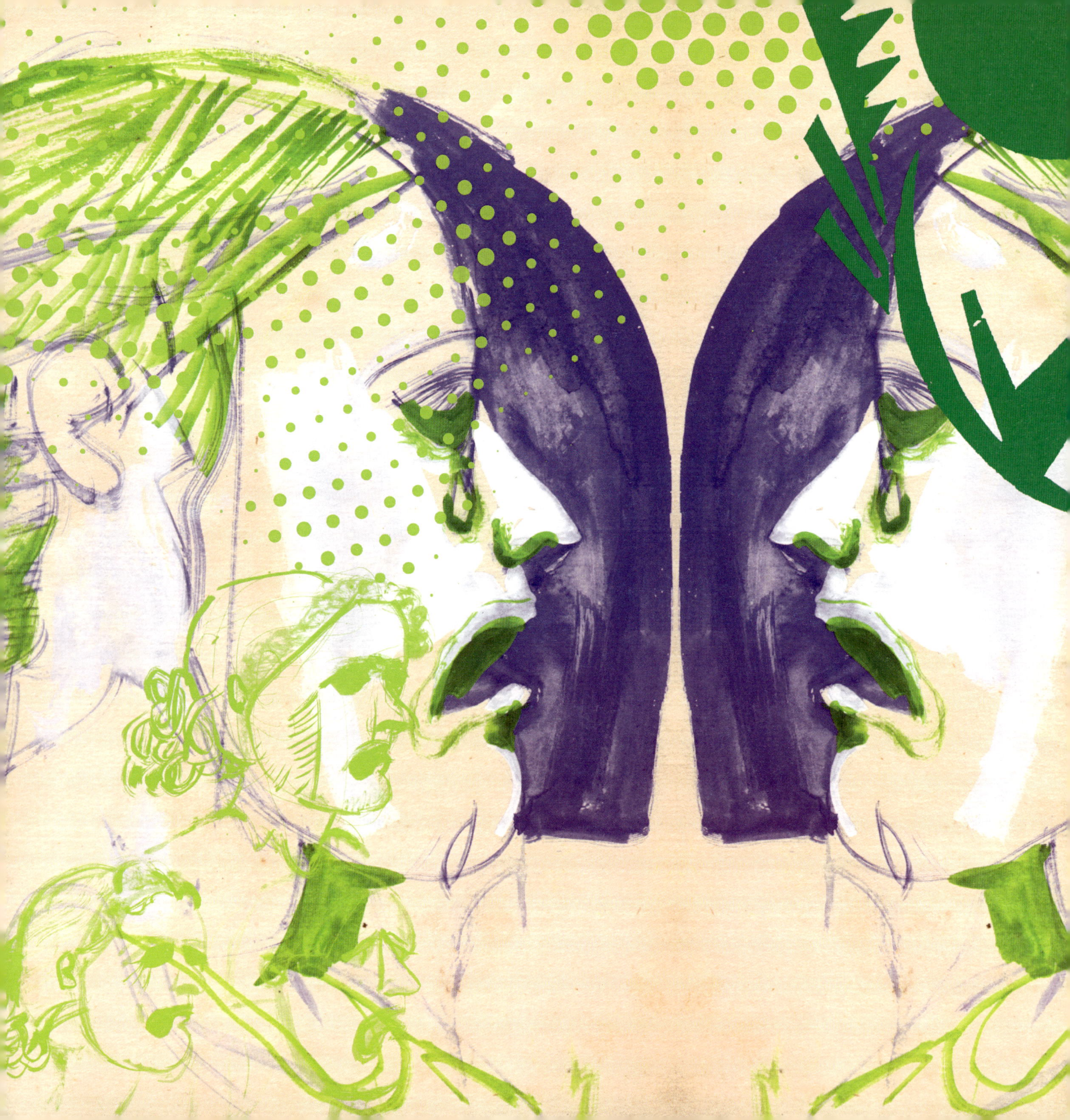

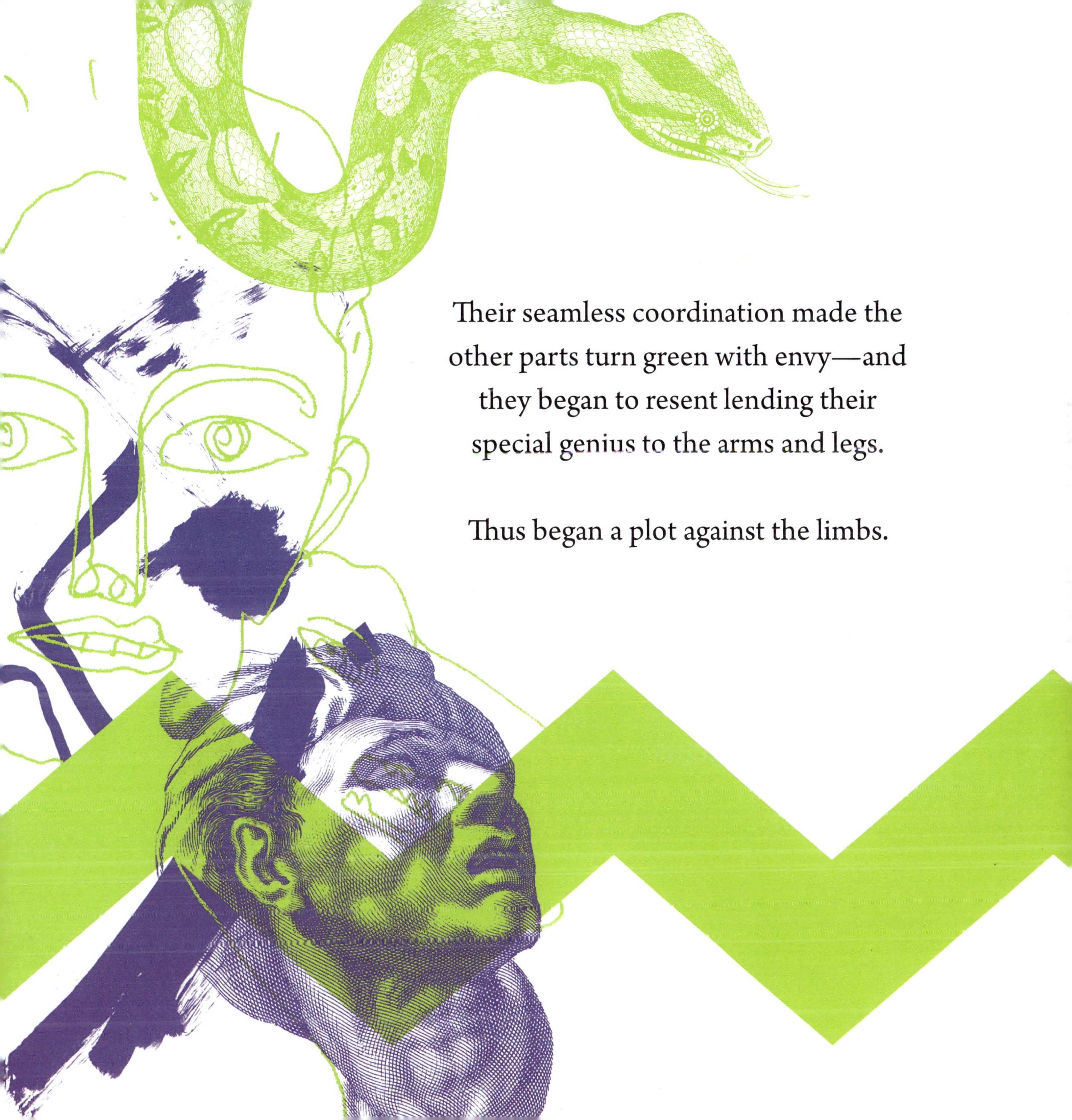

Their seamless coordination made the other parts turn green with envy—and they began to resent lending their special genius to the arms and legs.

Thus began a plot against the limbs.

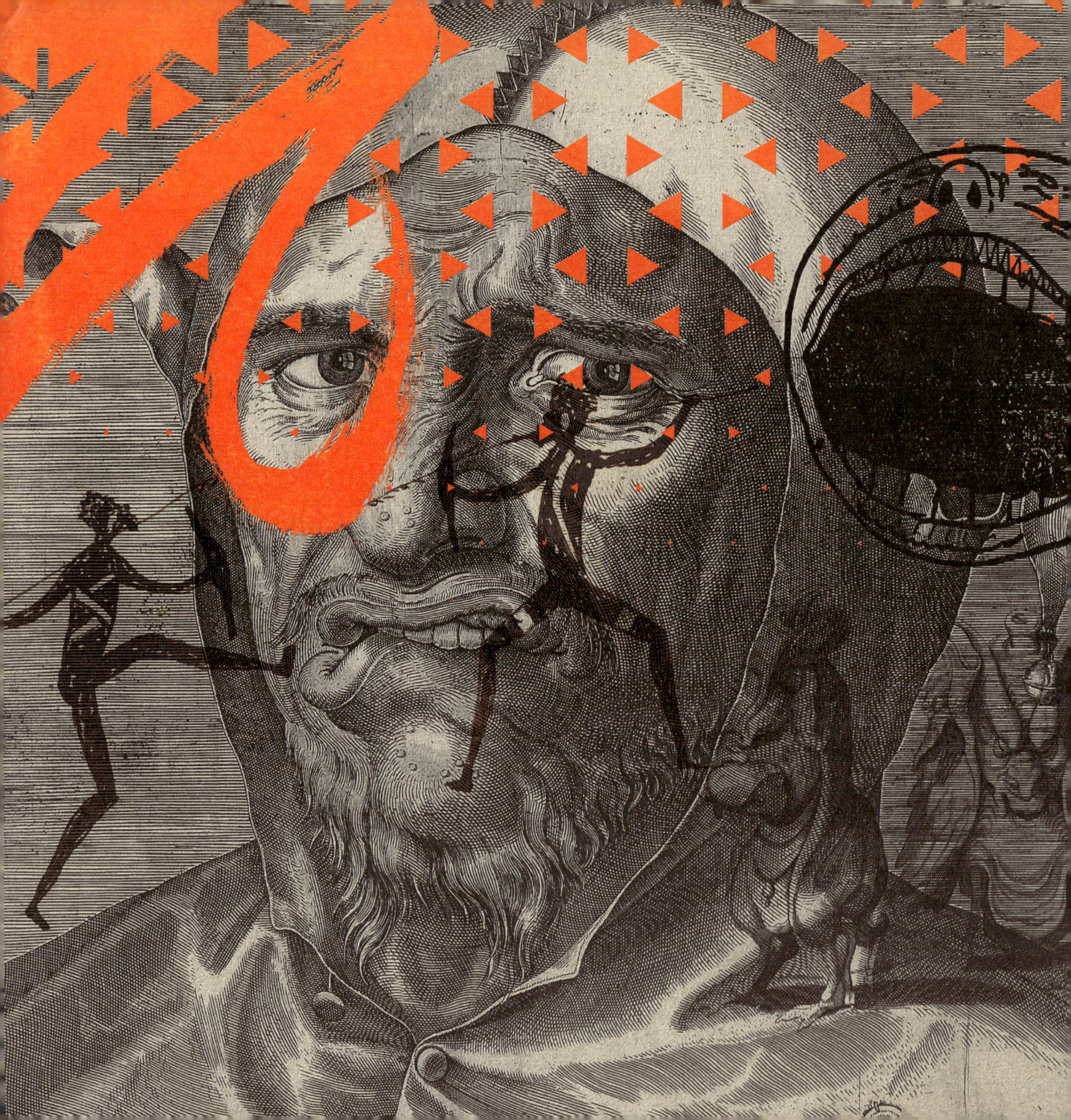

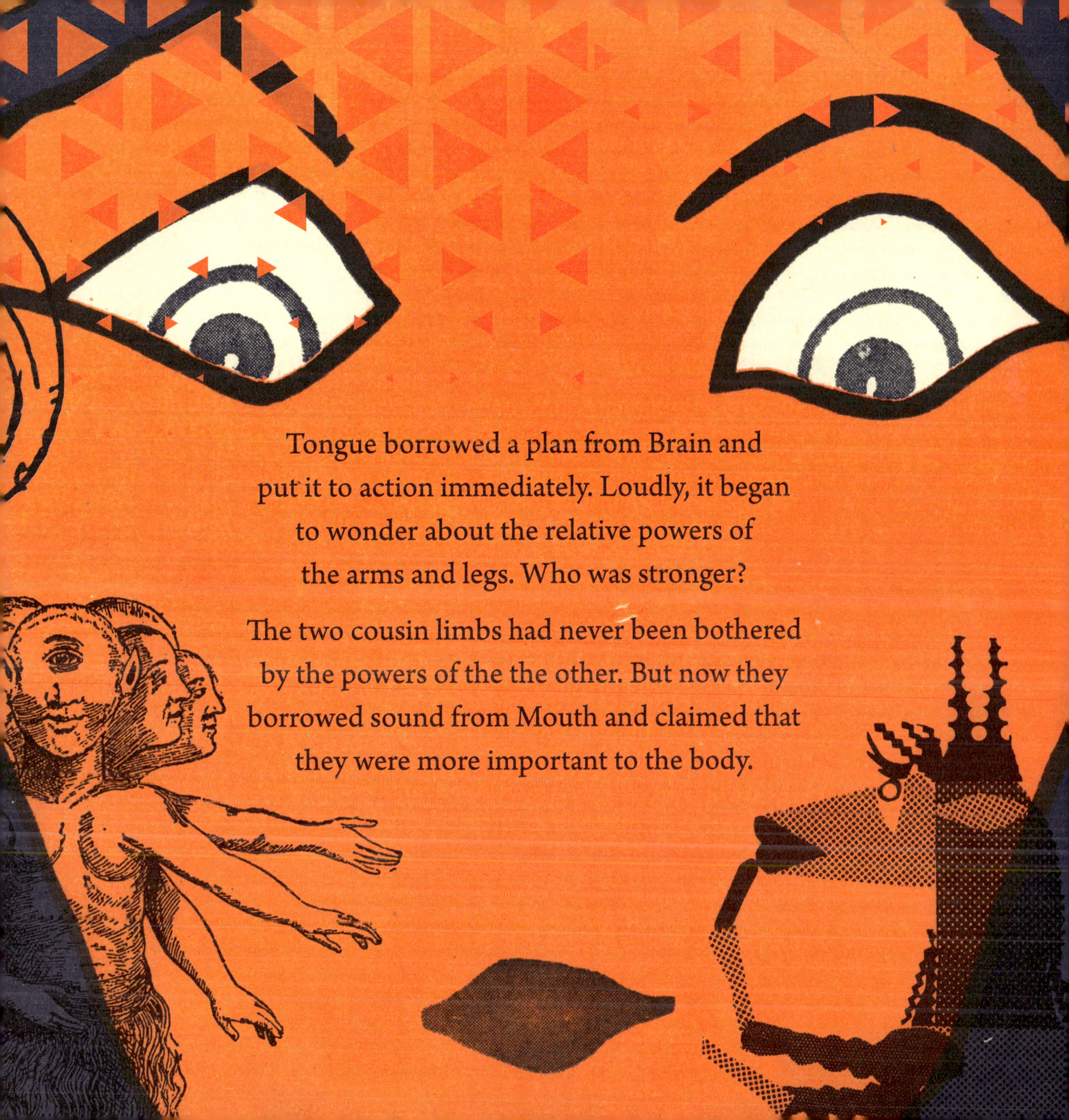

Tongue borrowed a plan from Brain and put it to action immediately. Loudly, it began to wonder about the relative powers of the arms and legs. Who was stronger?

The two cousin limbs had never been bothered by the powers of the the other. But now they borrowed sound from Mouth and claimed that they were more important to the body.

Soon a debate began about who was more elegant—arms bragged about the long slim fingers of its hands unlike the toes that were short and stout. Toes snapped back that the fingers were clearly starving, that's why they were so thin!

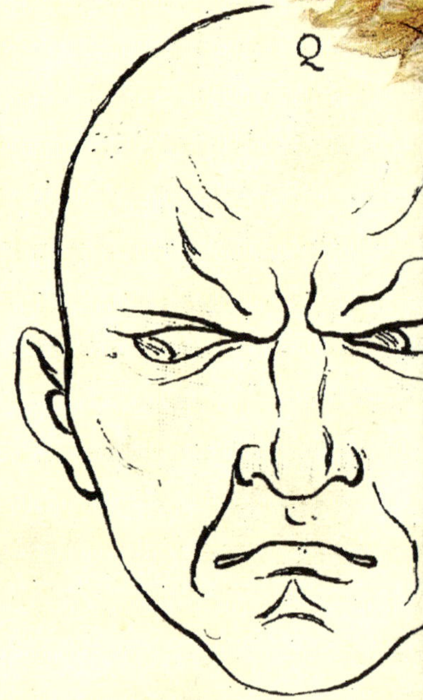

This went on for days, and of course began to affect their ability to work together.

It was Tongue who suggested a contest. A brilliant idea, everyone said. But what kind of contest?

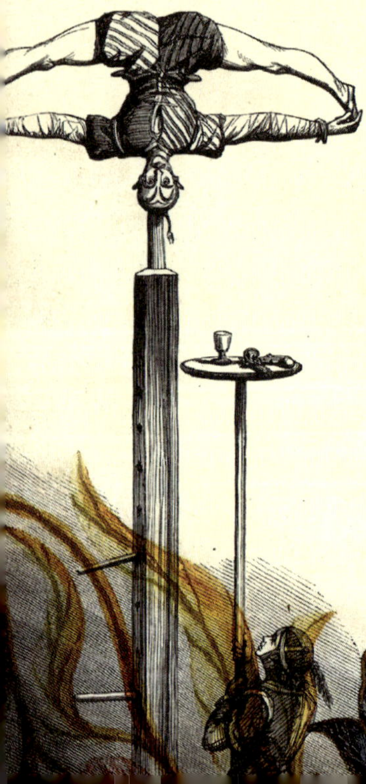

A wrestling match? Sword play, juggling, racing, or a game like chess or chequers? But each was unfair to one or other limb.

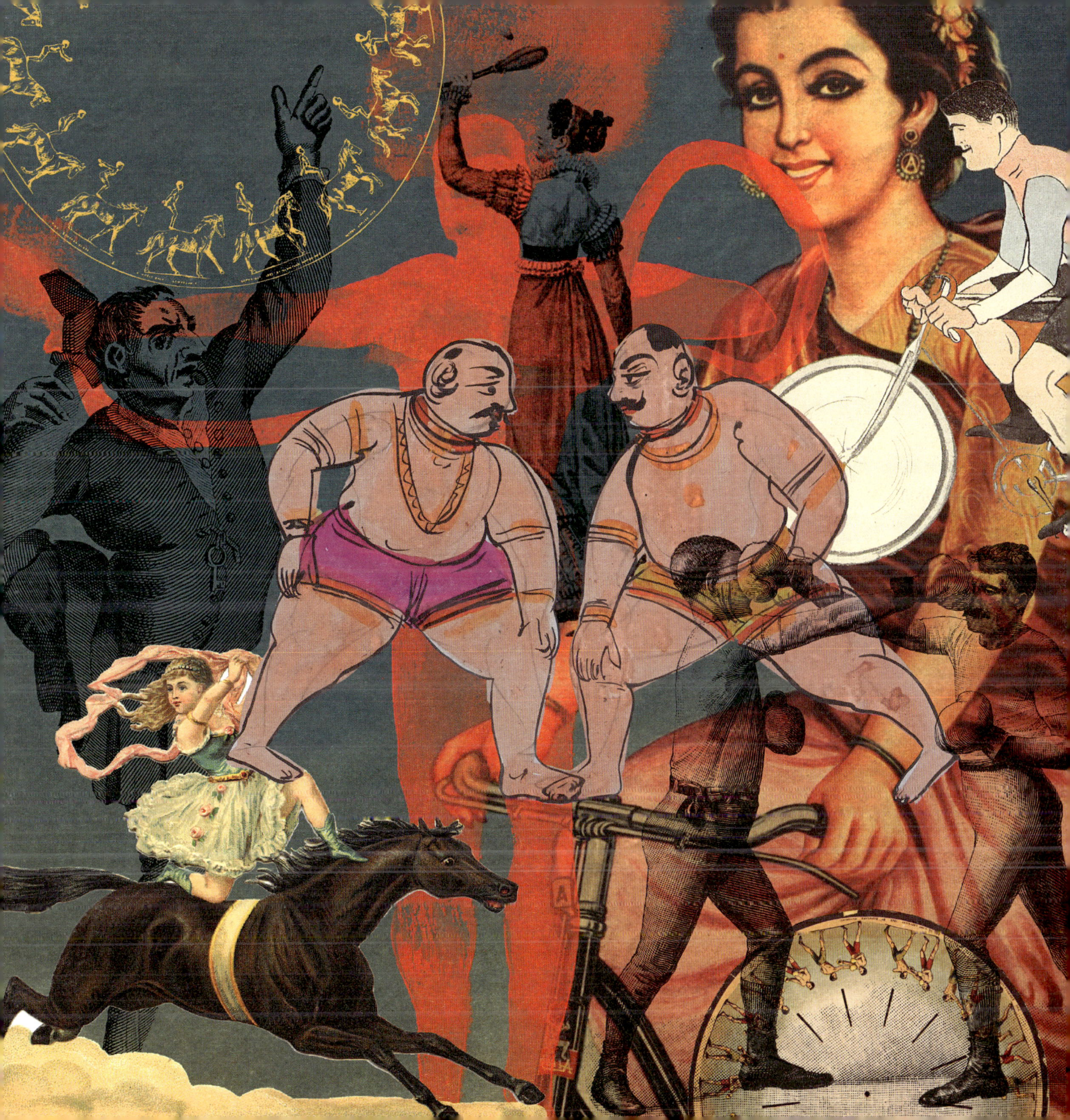

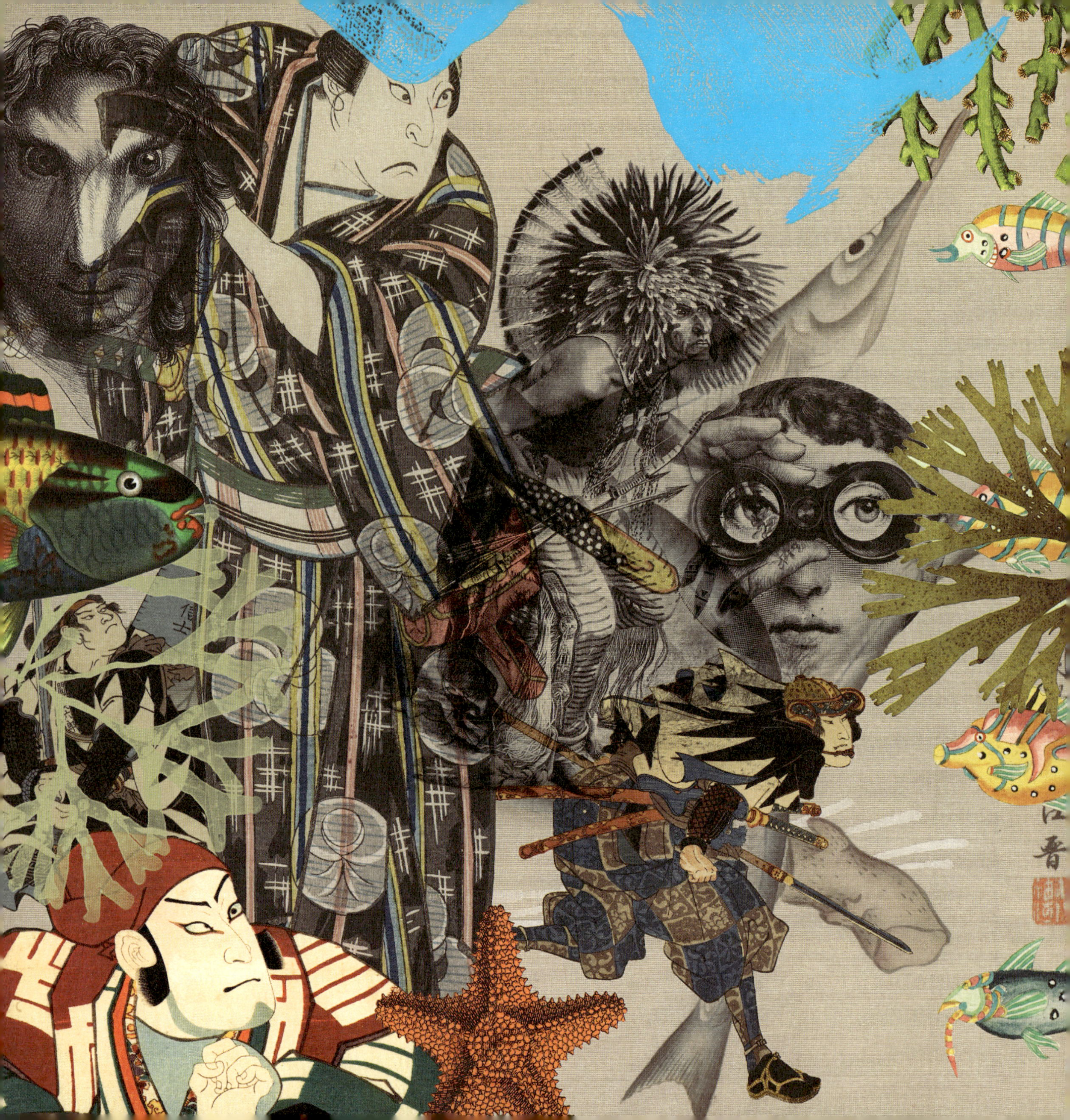

It was Tongue once again, after borrowing thought from Brain, who arrived at a simple solution: each set of organs would come up with a challenge.

Arms and Legs agreed.

The contest took place in a clearing in the forest, near a river. All the organs were on maximum alert for anything that might catch the body by surprise, now that they were engaged in internal struggle. Eyes scanned far and wide for the slightest threat; Ears primed themselves to hear the softest sound; Nose cleared its nostrils the better to detect the scent of danger; and Tongue was ready to shout: Beware!

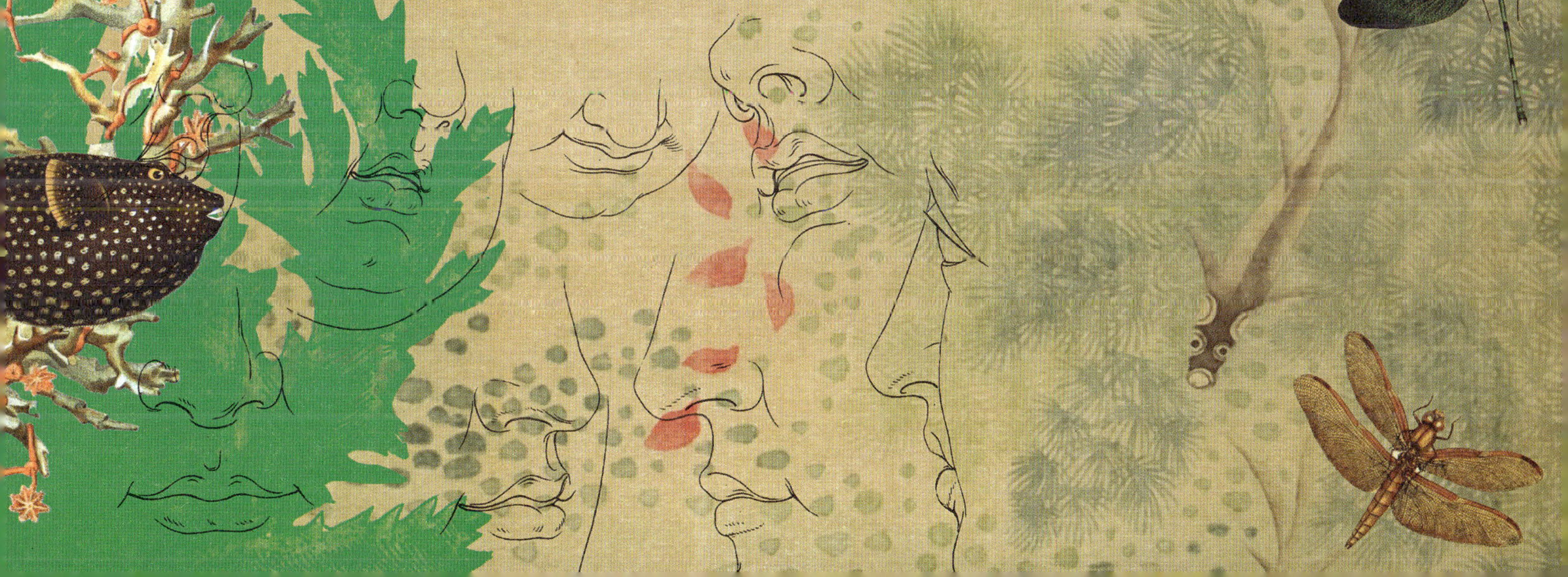

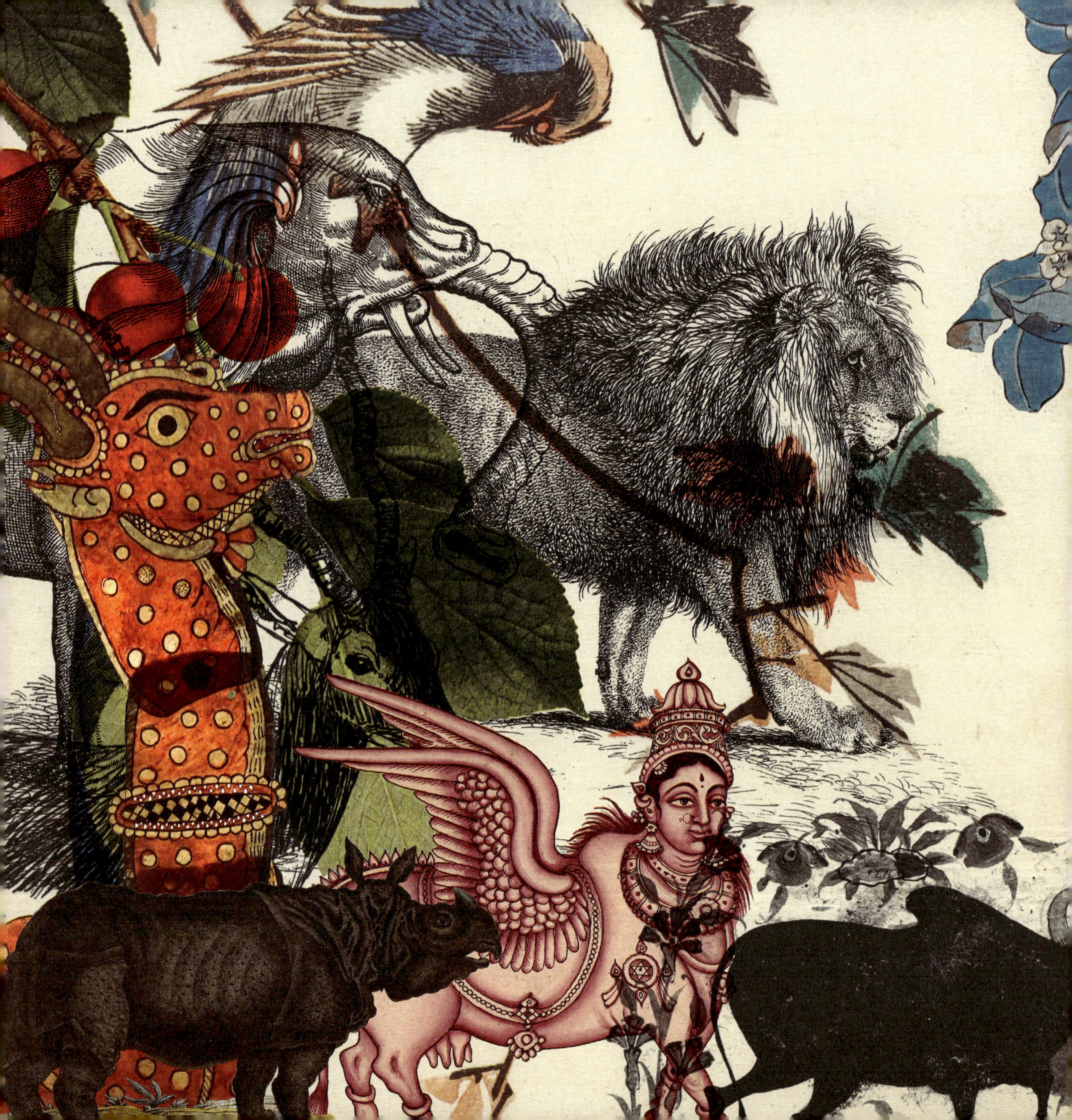

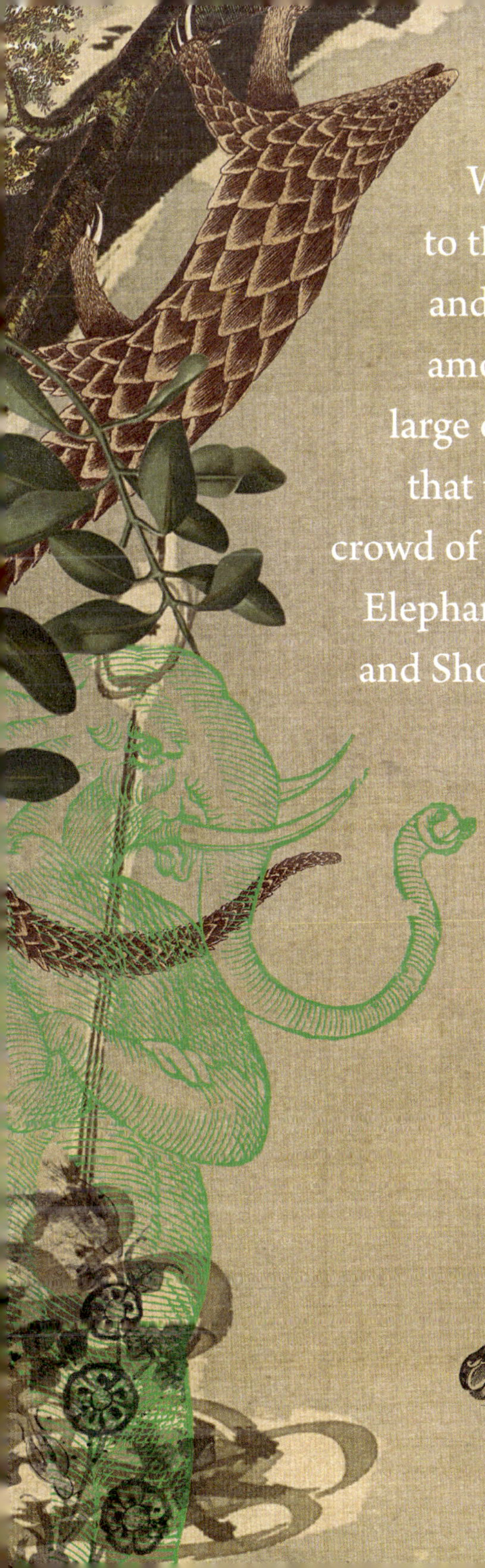

Wind spread news of the contest to the four corners of the forest, water and air. The four-legged animals were among the first to gather, many of the large ones holding green branches to show that they had come in peace, a colourful crowd of Leopard, Cheetah, Lion, Rhino, Hyena, Elephant, Giraffe, Camel, Long-Horned Cow and Short-Horned Buffalo, Antelope, Gazelle, Hare, Mole and Rat.

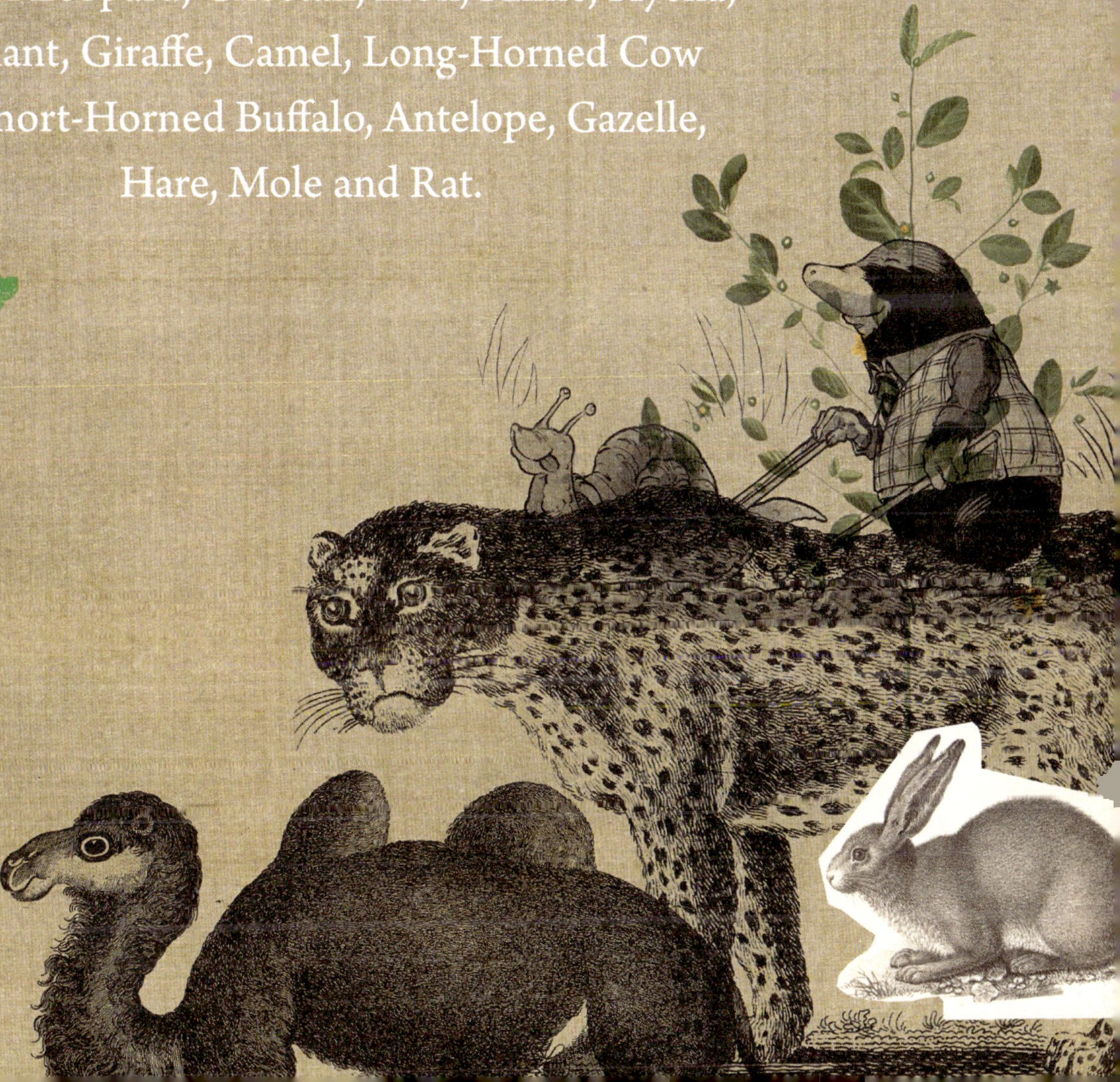

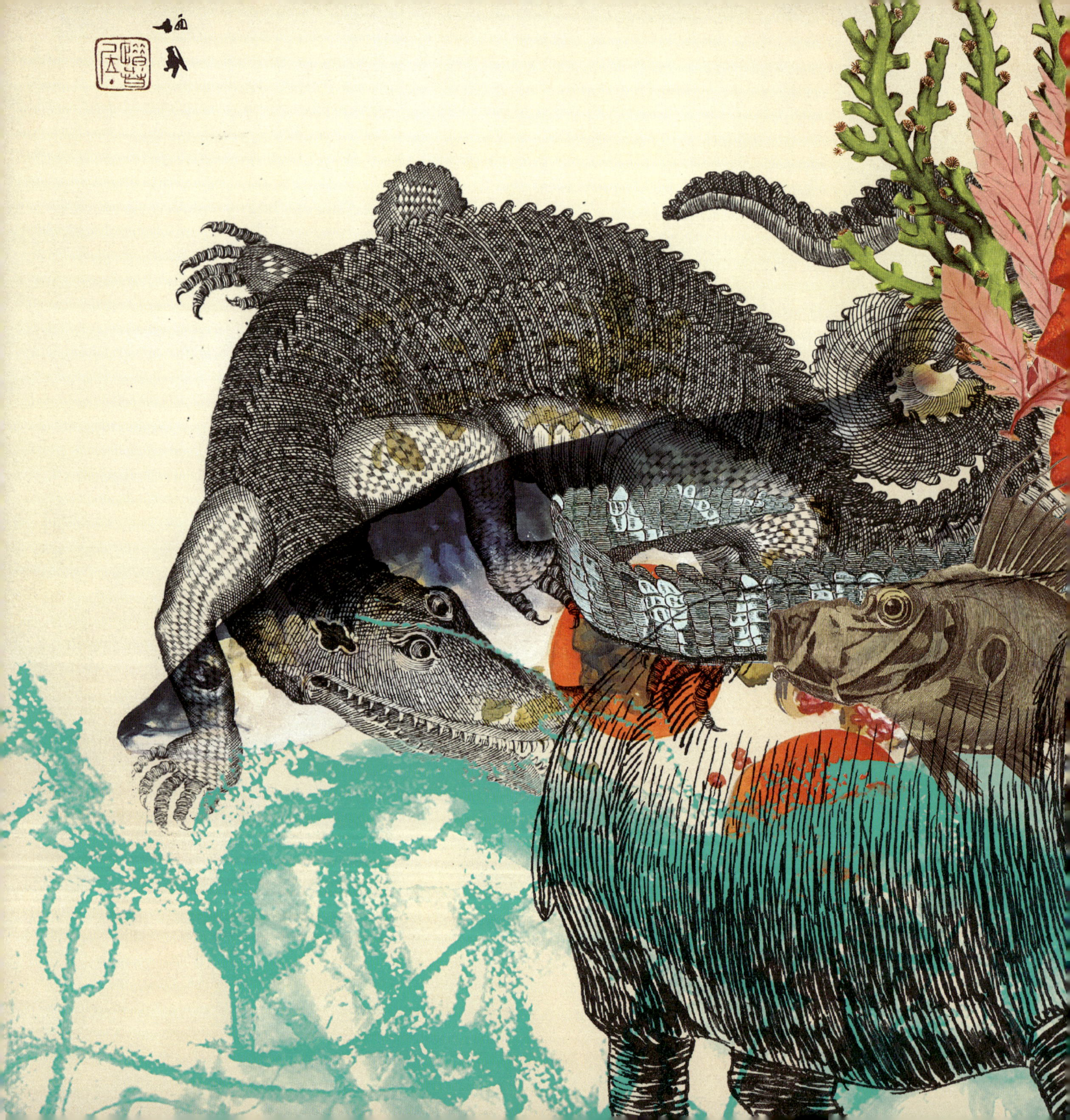

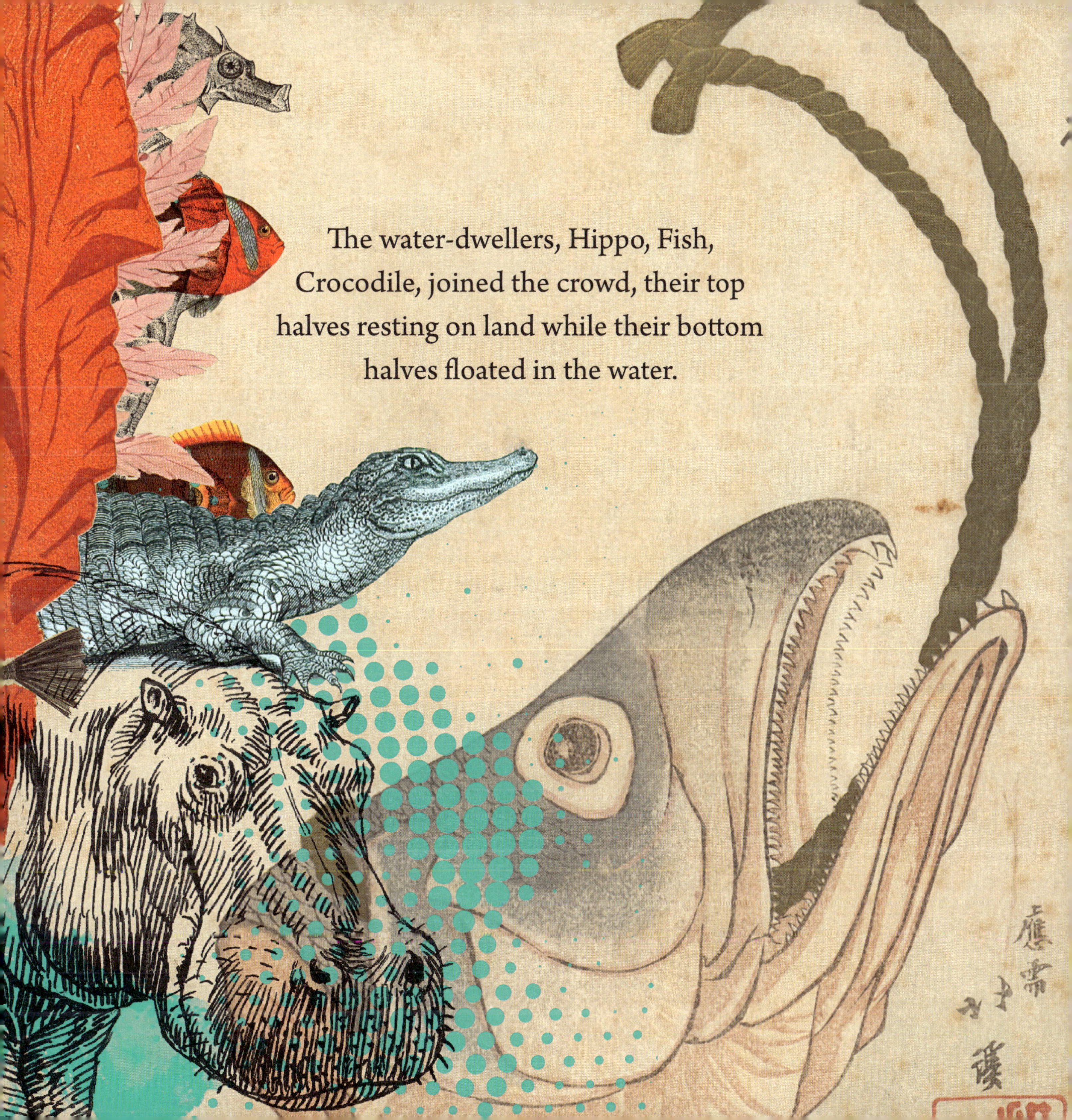

The water-dwellers, Hippo, Fish, Crocodile, joined the crowd, their top halves resting on land while their bottom halves floated in the water.

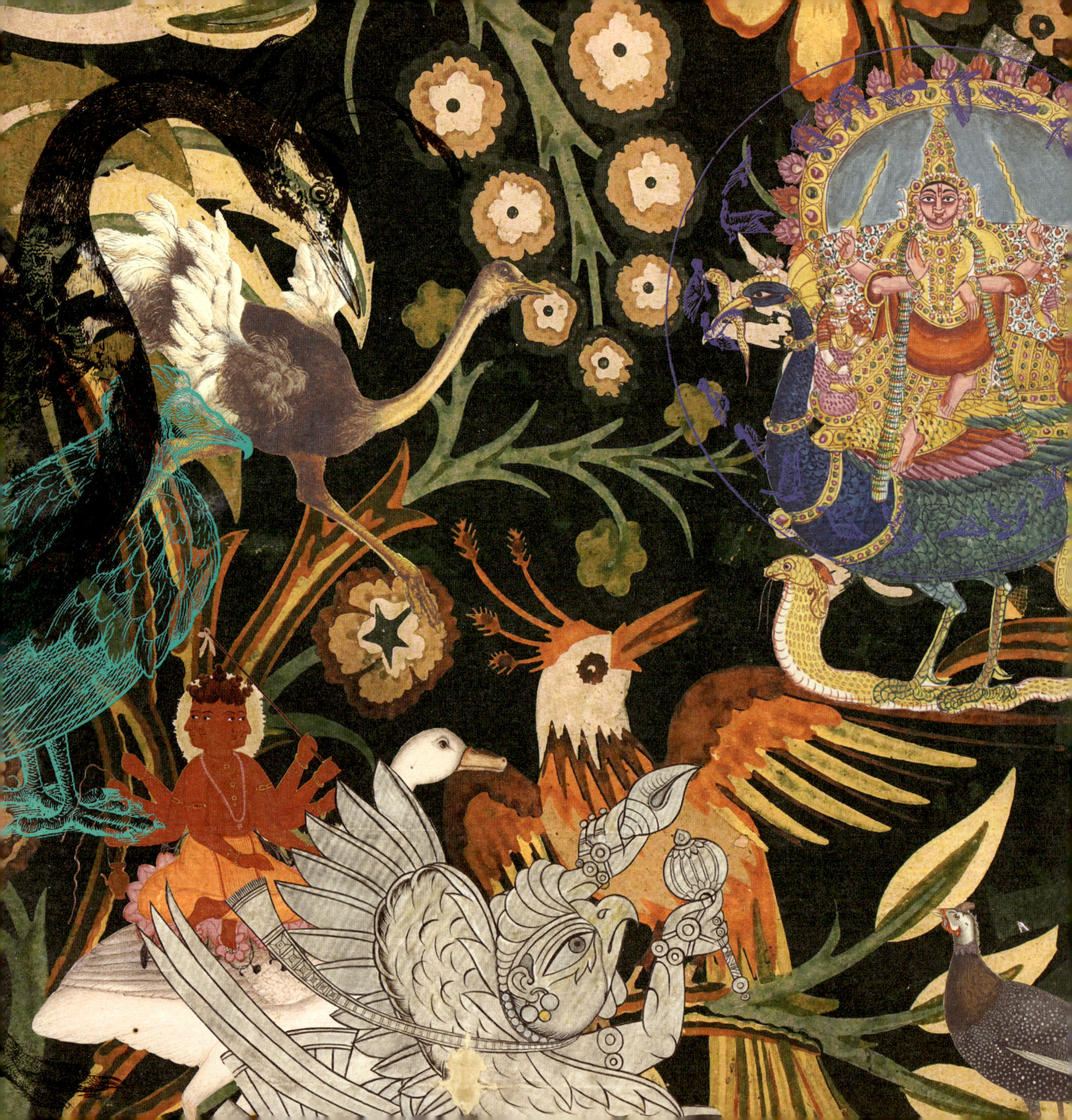

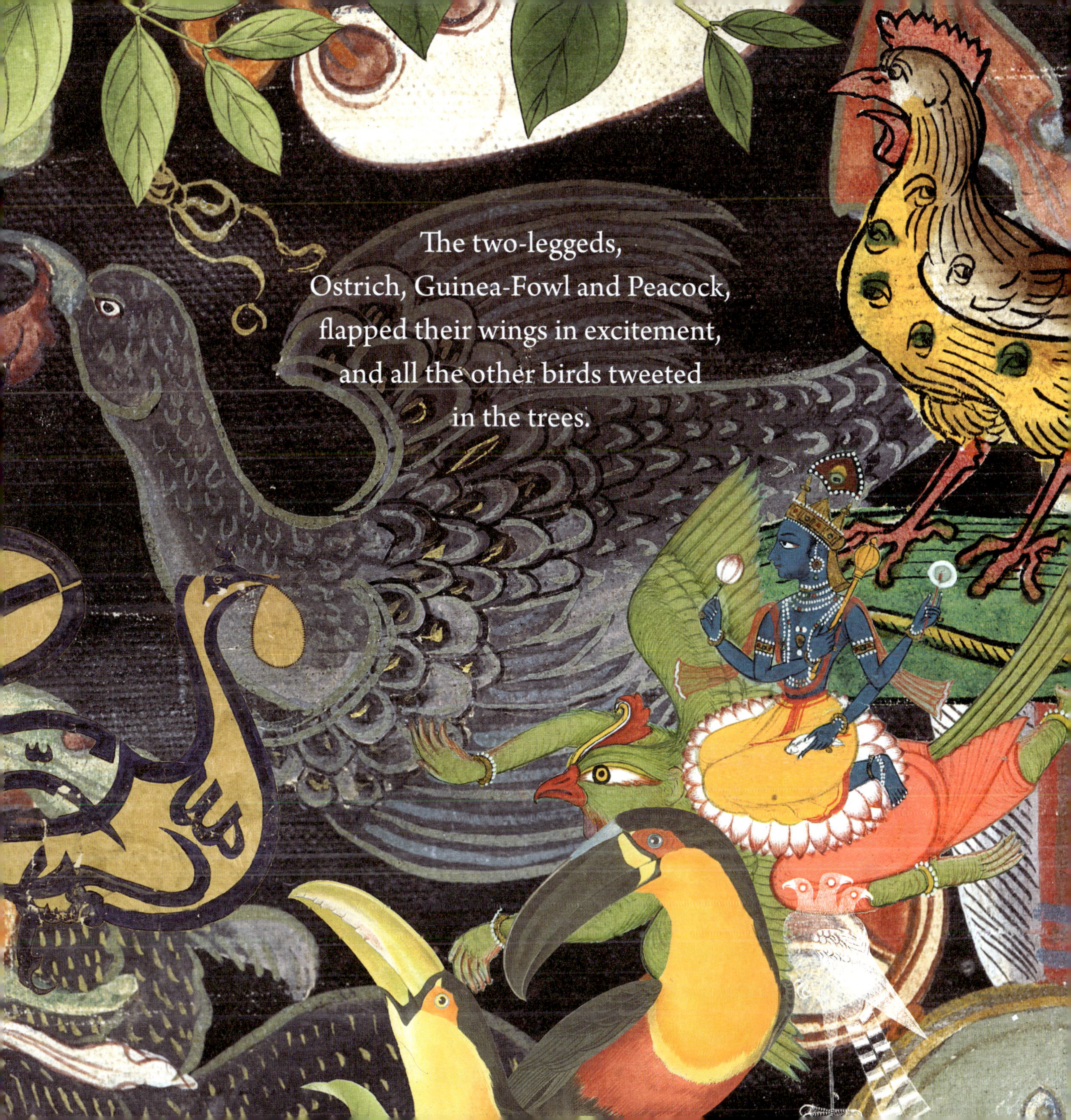

The two-leggeds,
Ostrich, Guinea-Fowl and Peacock,
flapped their wings in excitement,
and all the other birds tweeted
in the trees.

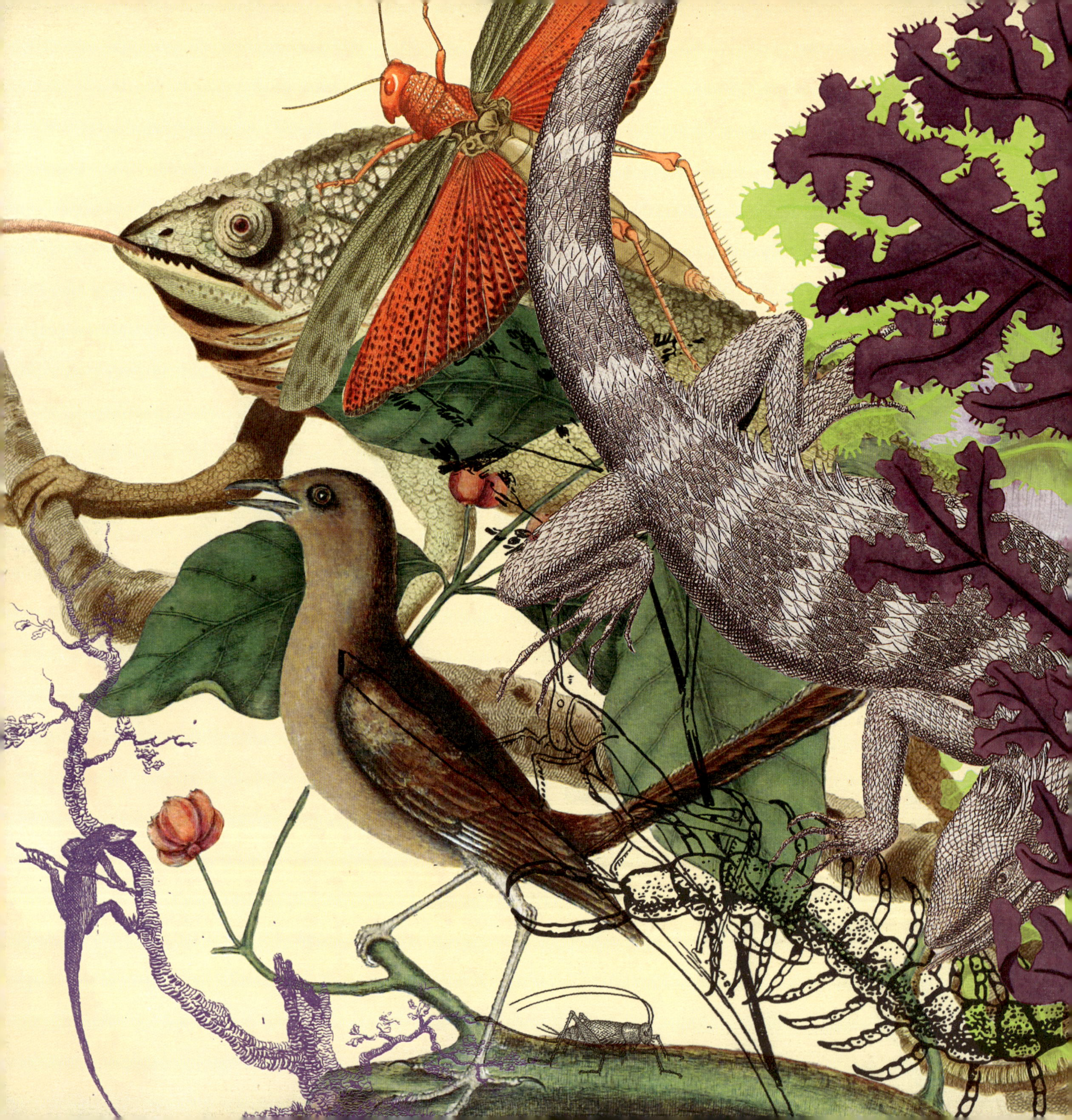

Cricket sang all the time. Spider, Worm, Centipede, Millipede crawled about on the ground or trees. Chameleon walked stealthily, carefully, taking its time while Lizard ran about, refusing to settle down in one spot.

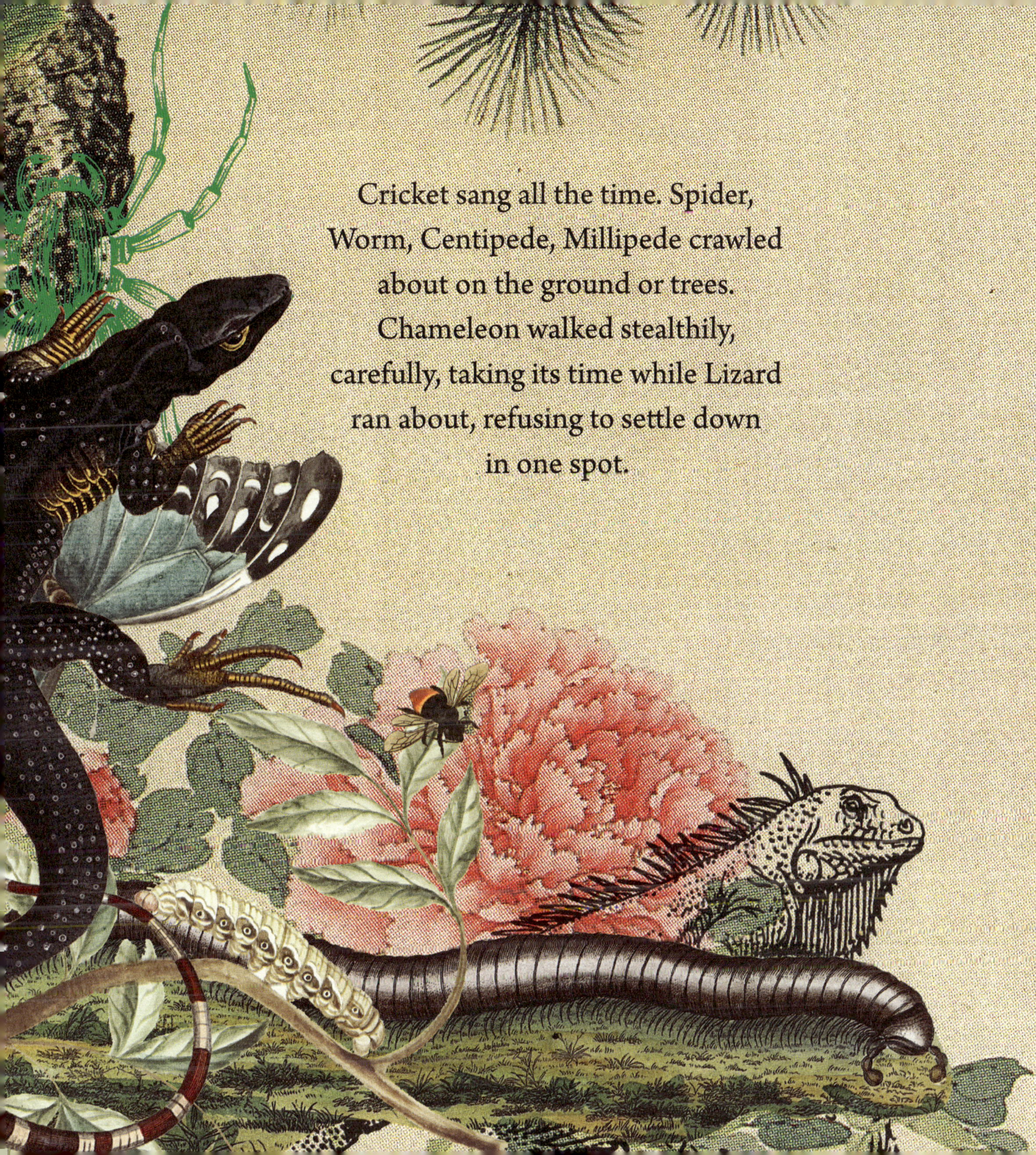

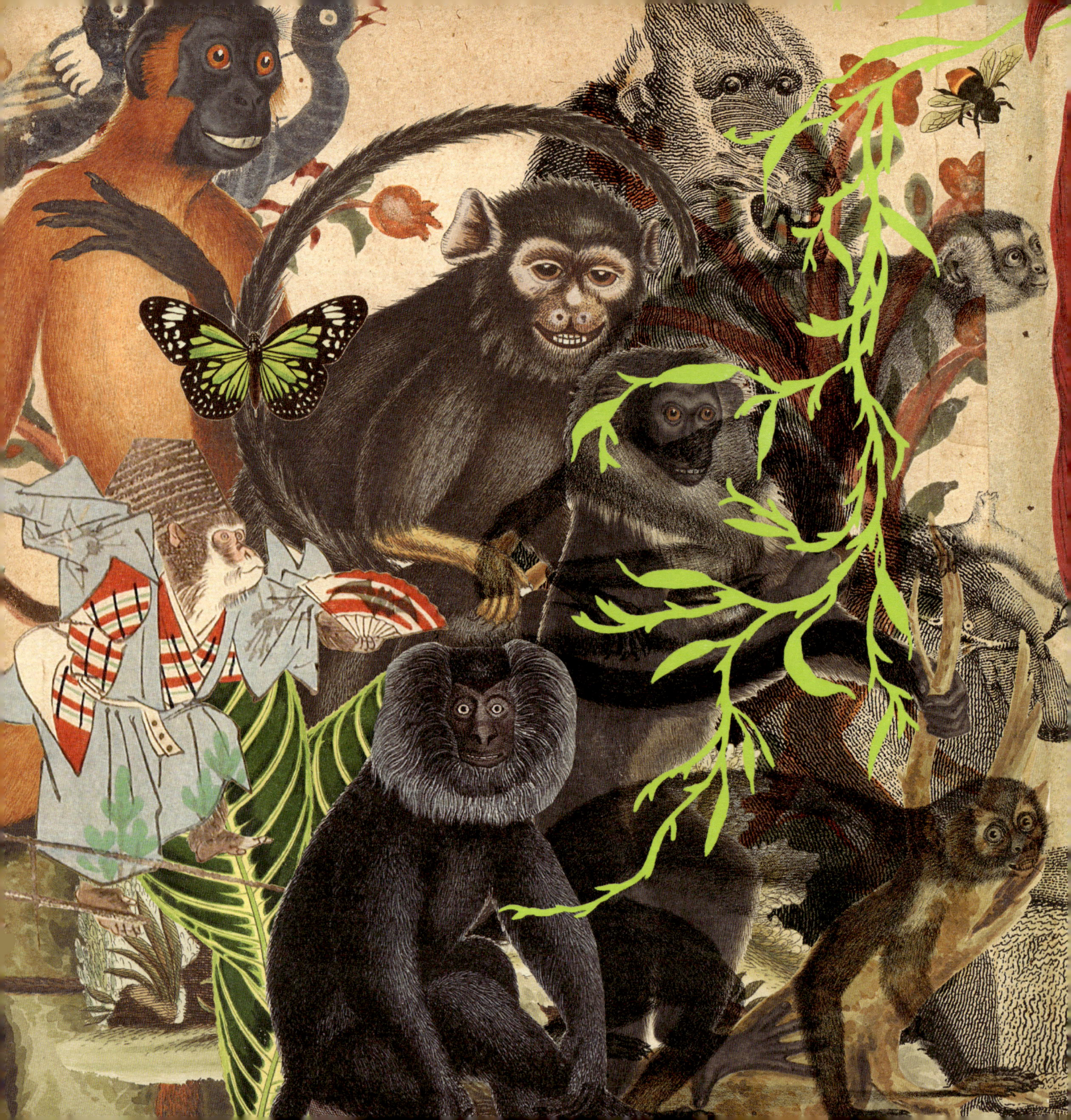

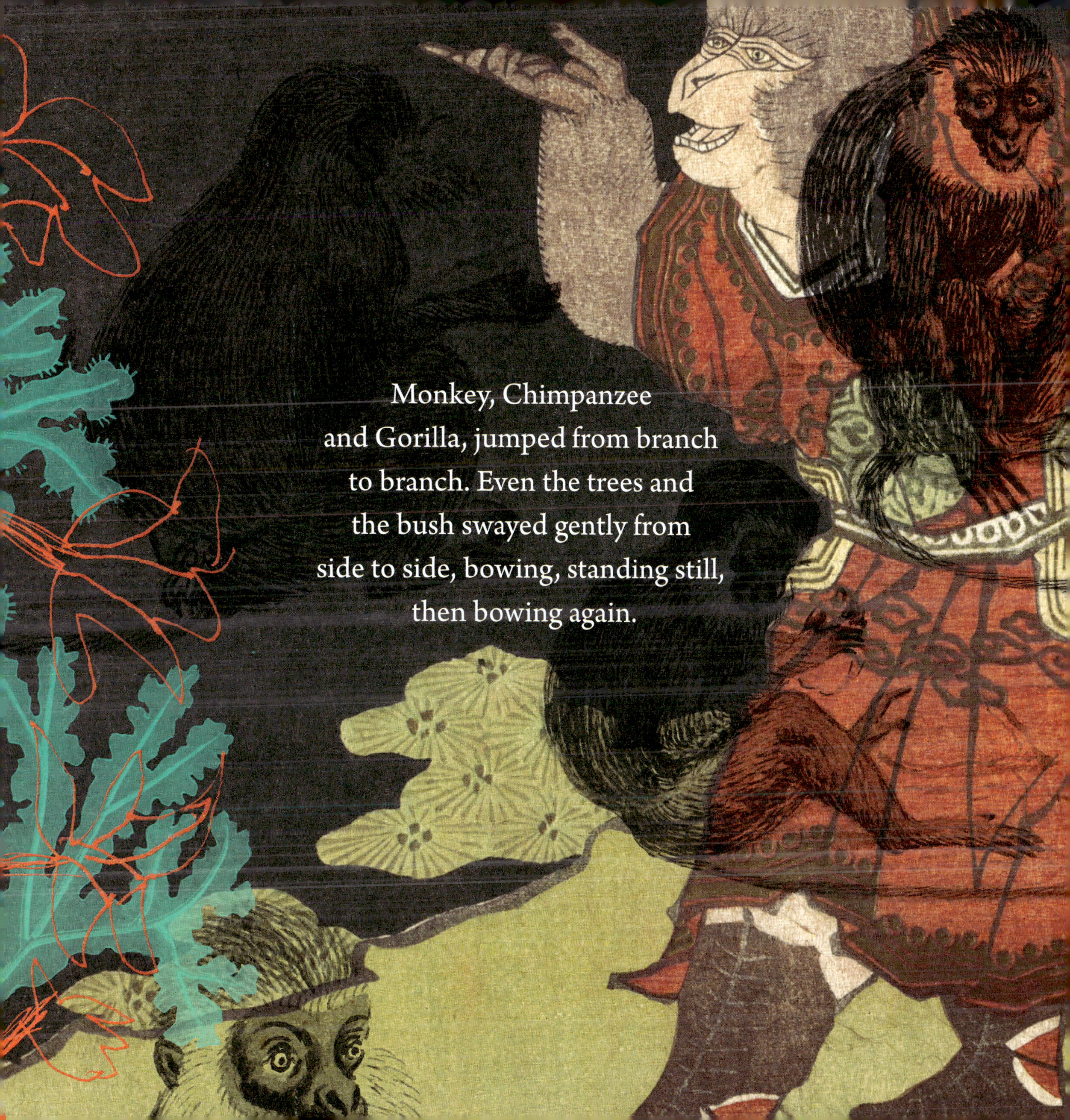

Monkey, Chimpanzee
and Gorilla, jumped from branch
to branch. Even the trees and
the bush swayed gently from
side to side, bowing, standing still,
then bowing again.

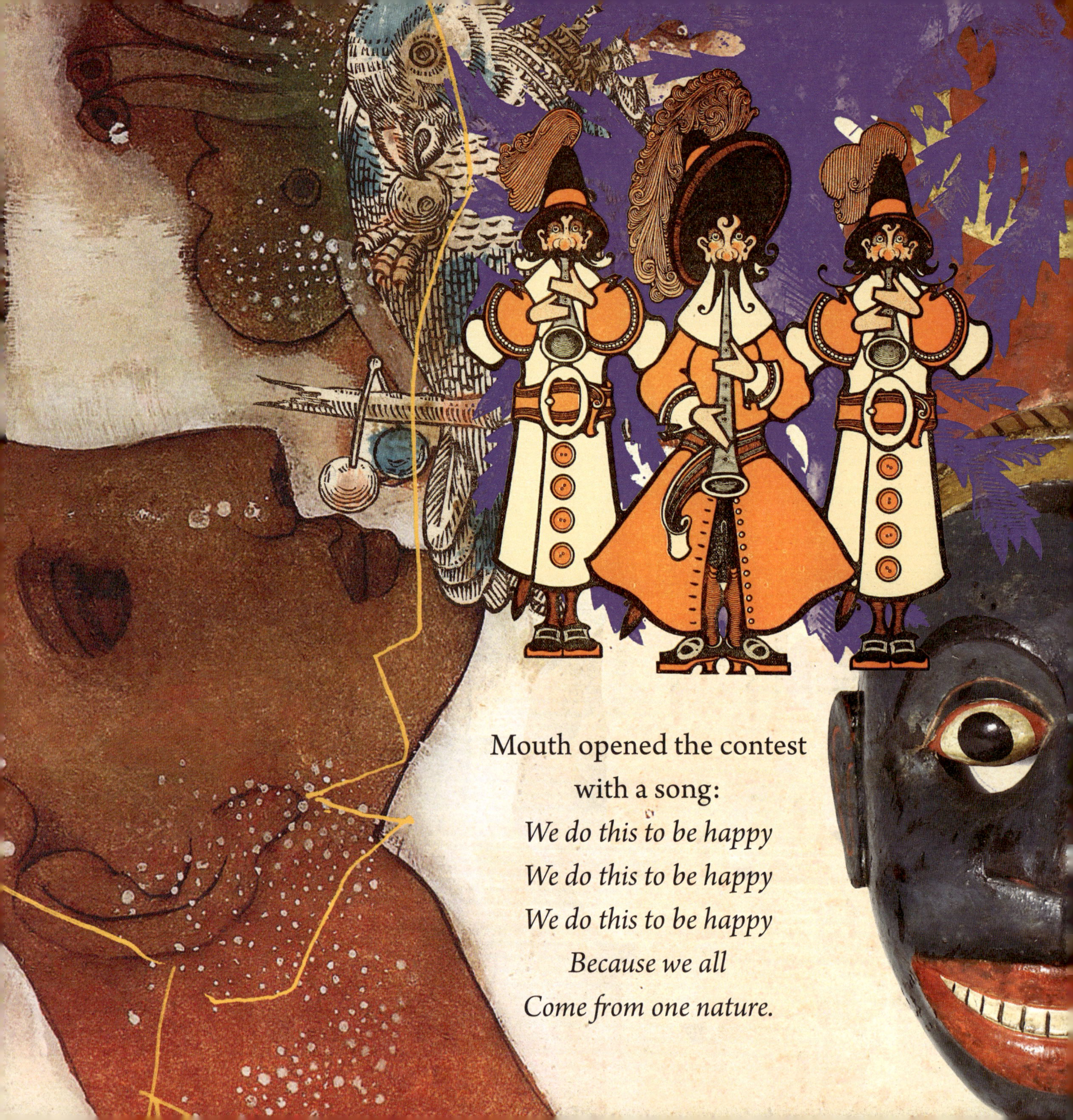

Mouth opened the contest
with a song:
We do this to be happy
We do this to be happy
We do this to be happy
Because we all
Come from one nature.

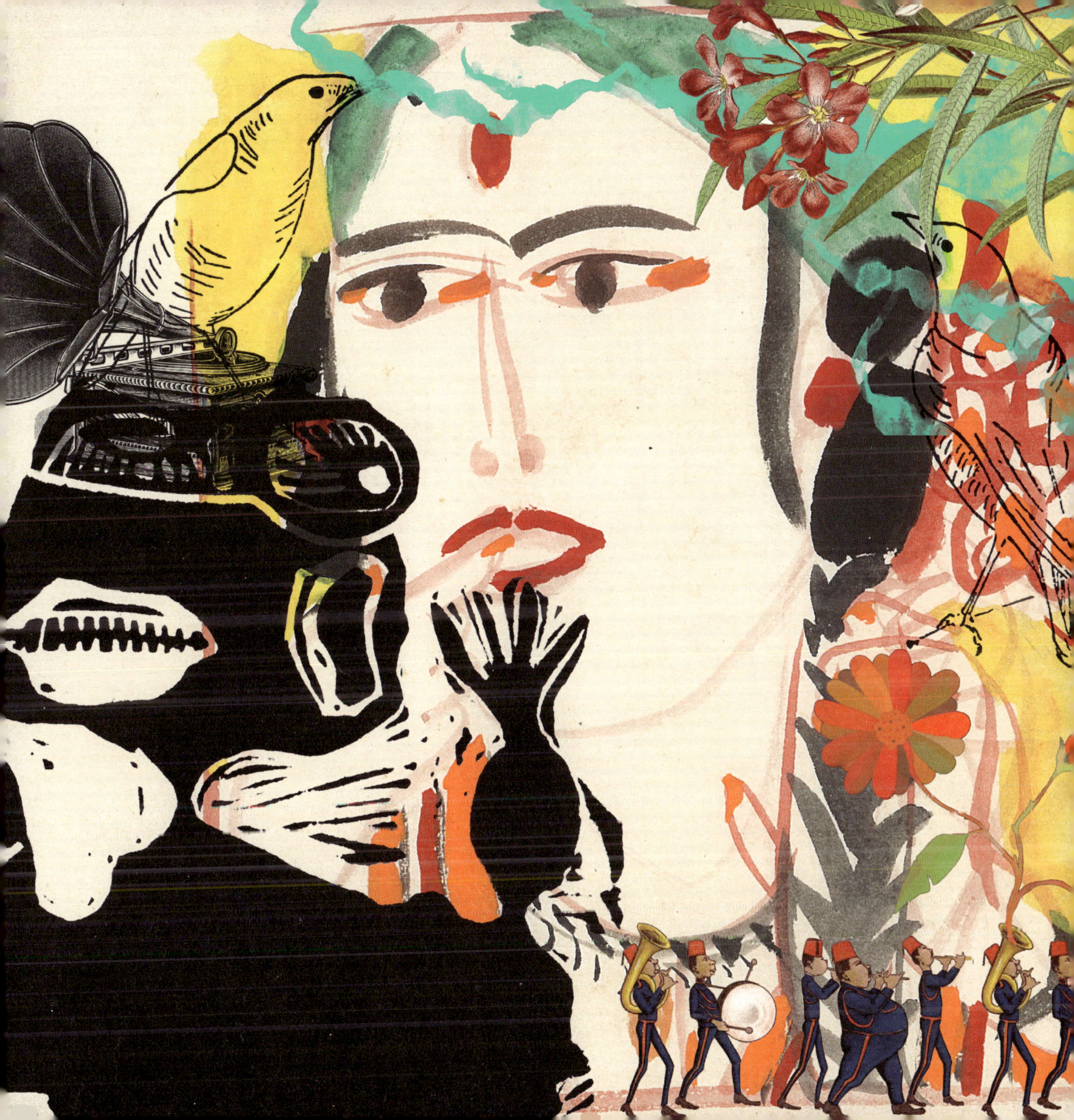

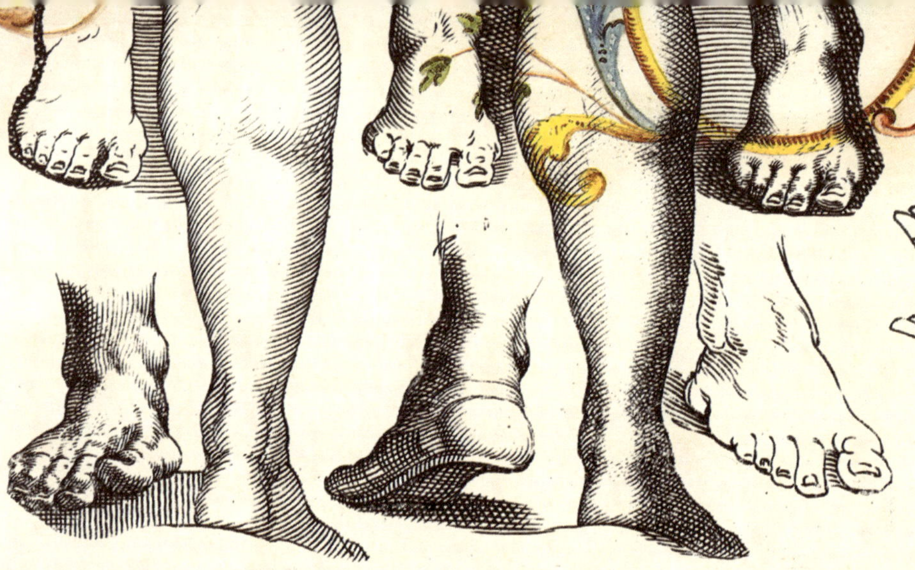

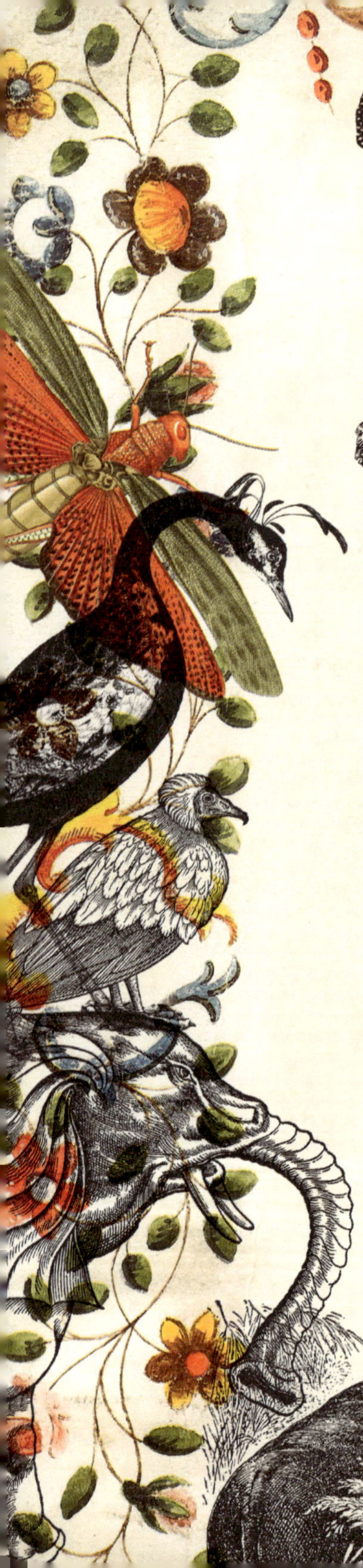

Arms issued their challenge: Legs had to pick up a piece of wood from the ground and throw it. Legs got to work—they tried to turn over the piece of wood, to push it . . . but they simply could not pick it up. All they could do was kick it a few inches away.

Seeing them struggle, Fingers borrowed sound from Mouth and laughed and laughed. And Arms strutted about before the audience, preening and showing off their slim looks.

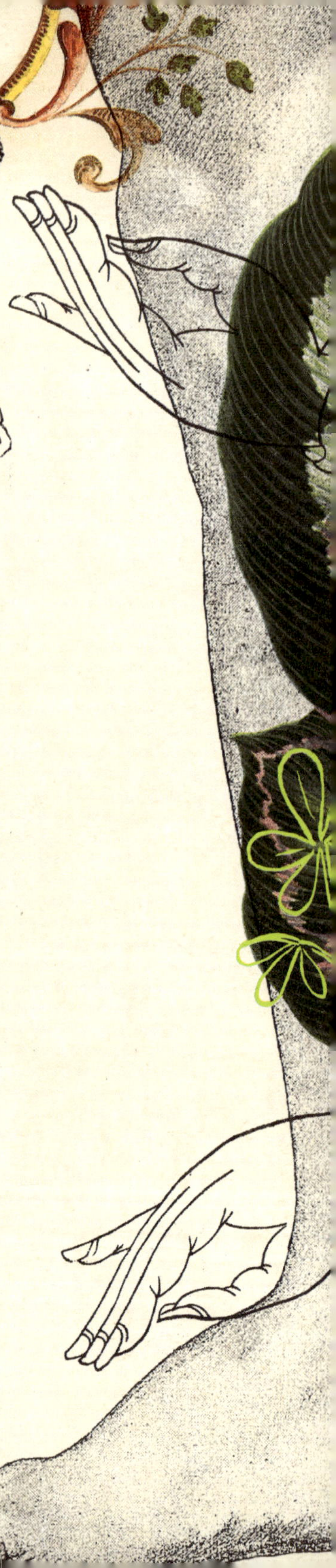

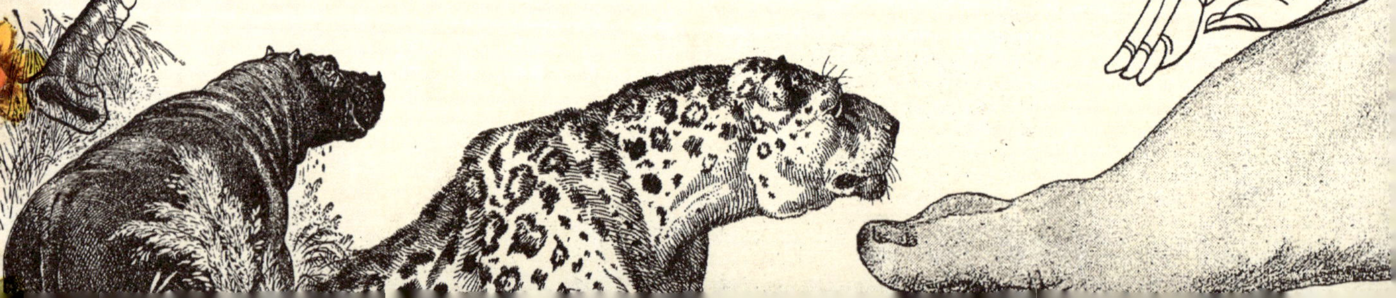

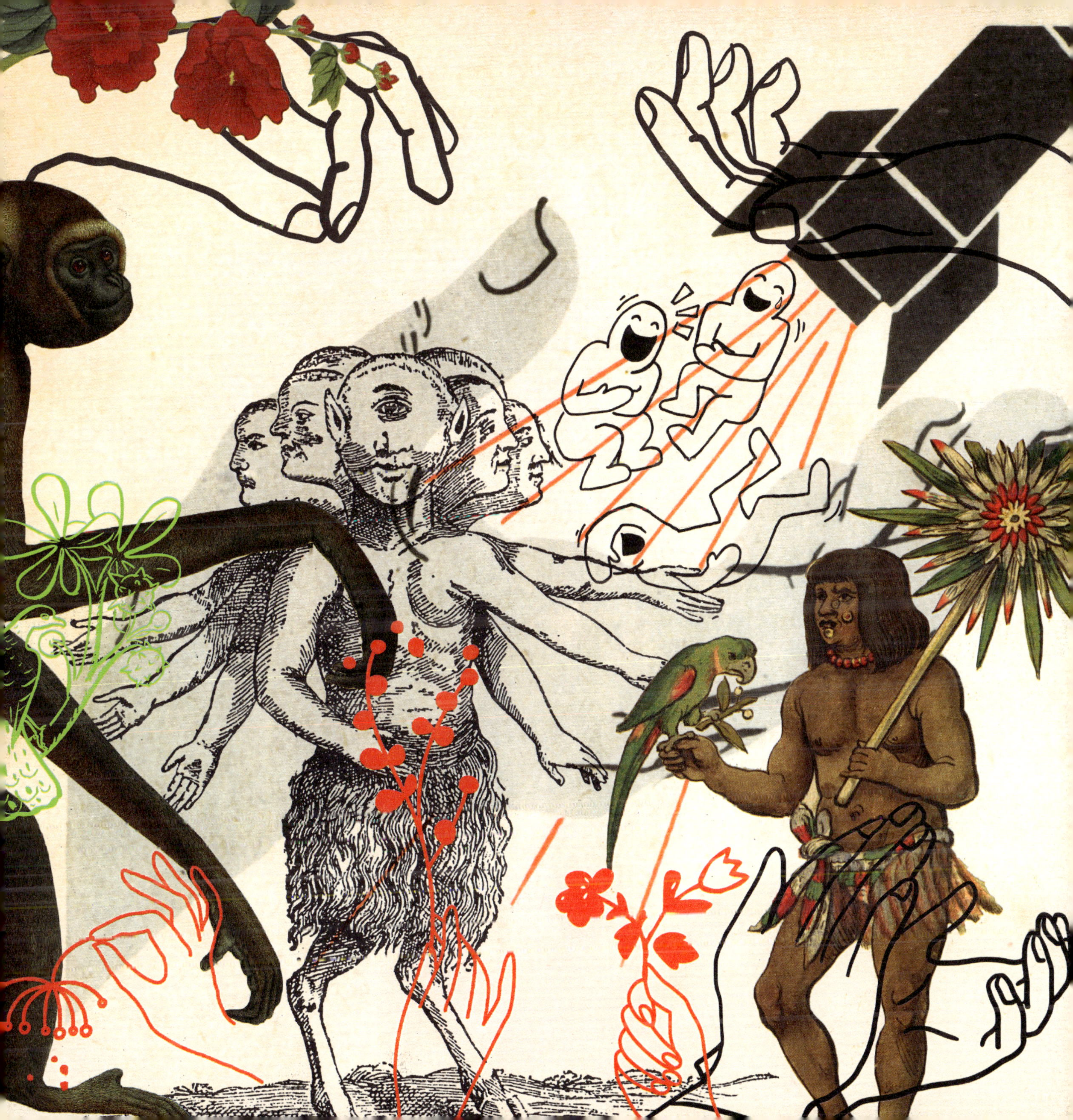

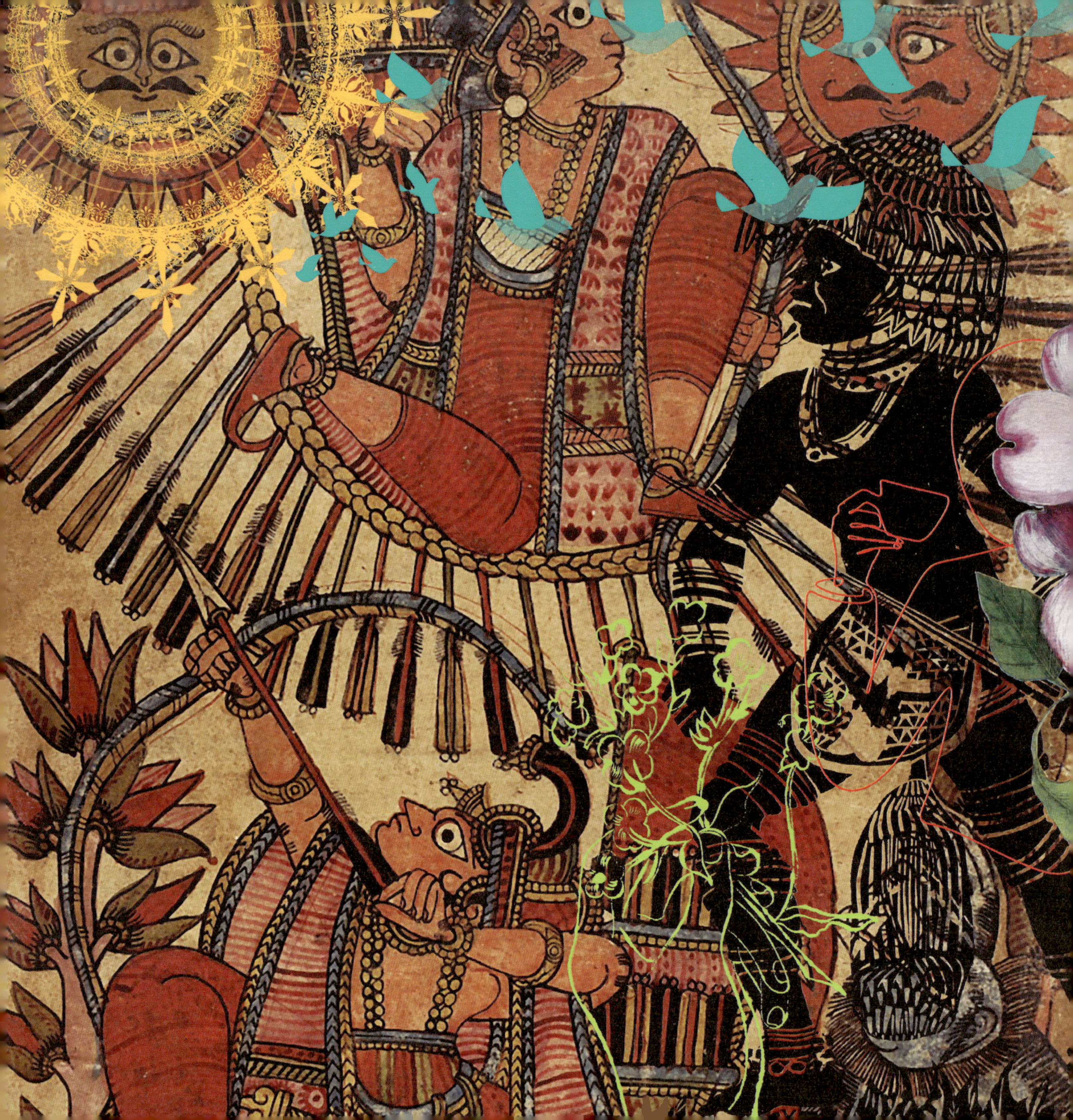

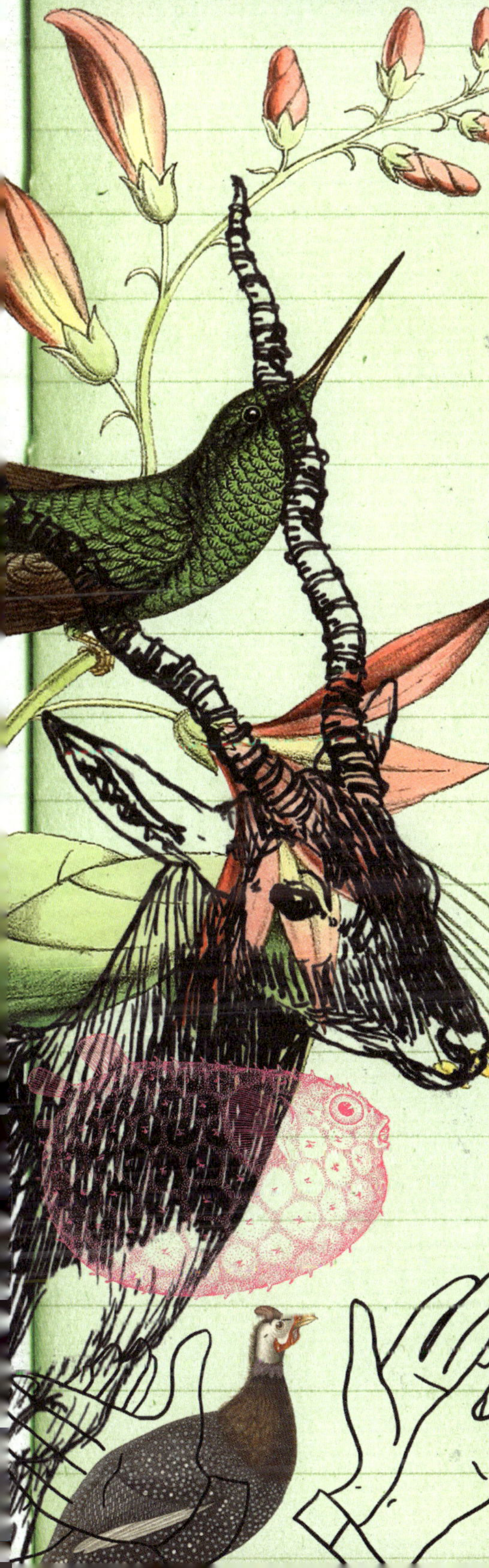

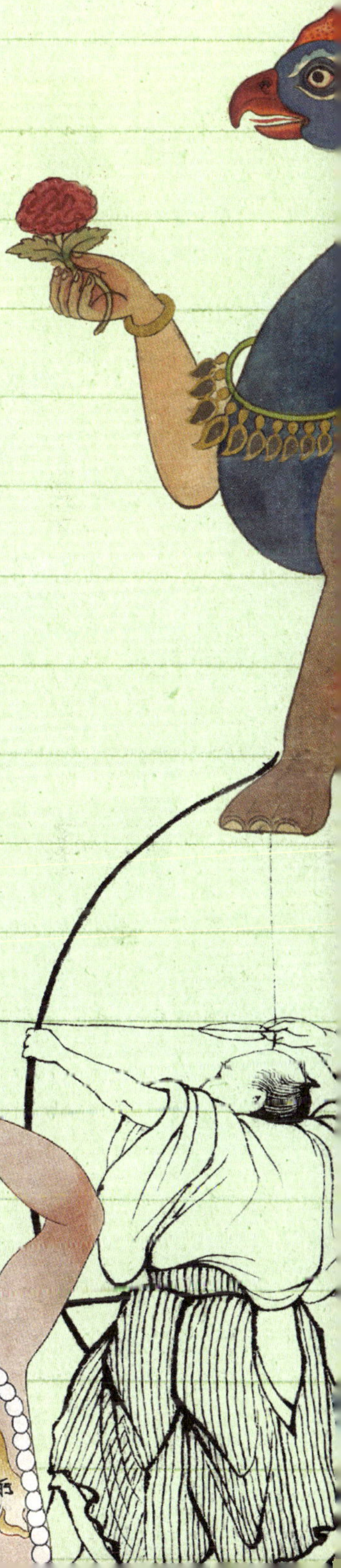

Then Fingers picked up the piece of wood and threw it far into the forest, eliciting a sigh of admiration from both contestants and spectators. Then they picked out bits of sand from a bowl of rice; threaded needles; made small pulleys for lifting heavy pieces of wood; made spears and hurled them into the distance.

The spectators' Hands clapped like thunder in solidarity and appreciation which upset Legs a great deal who were stumped by this display of dexterity.

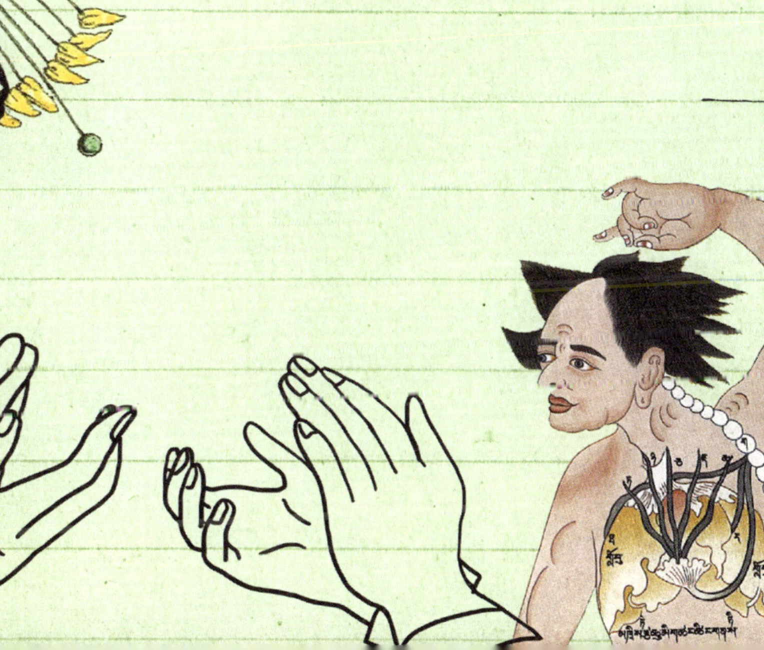

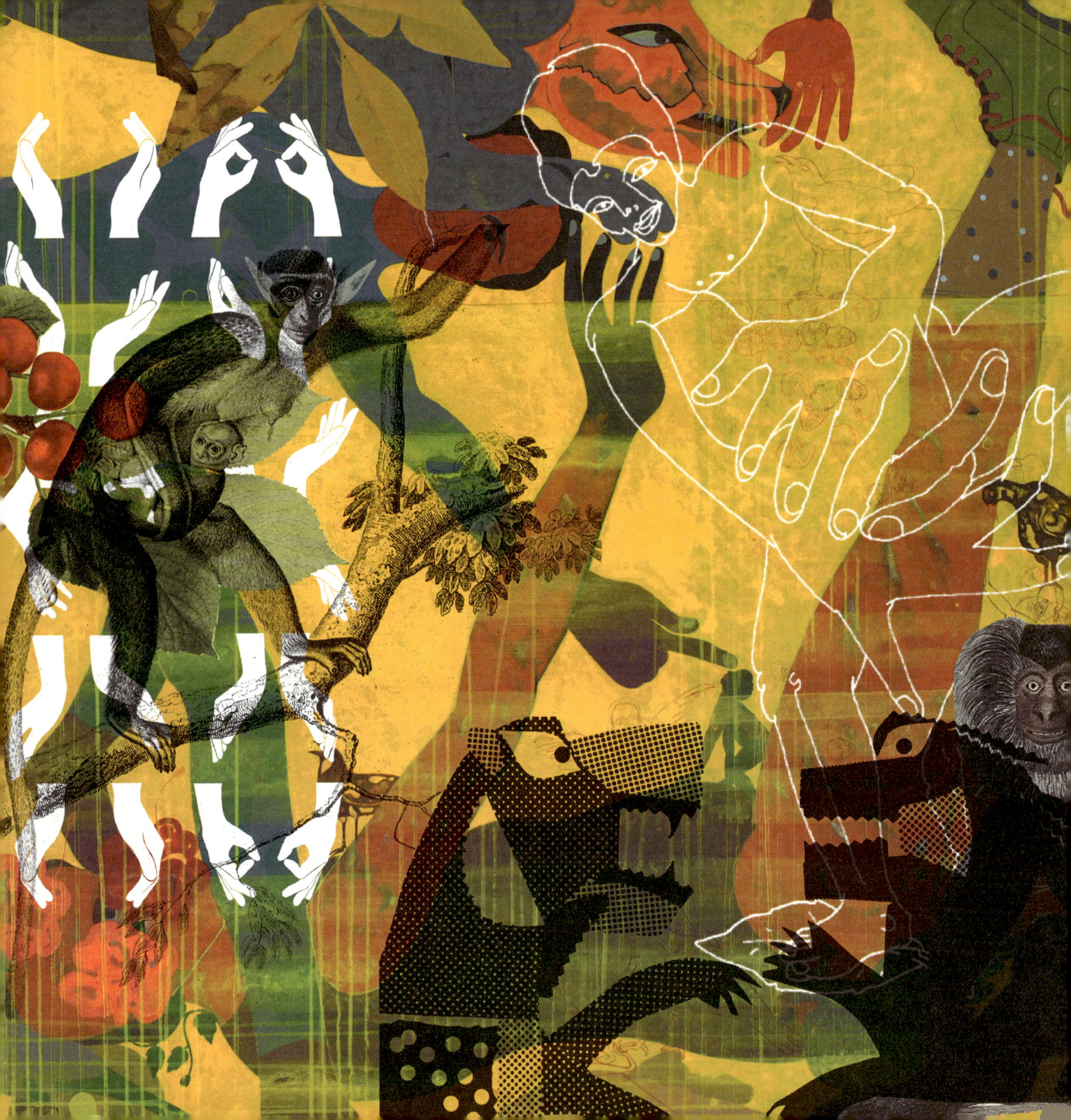

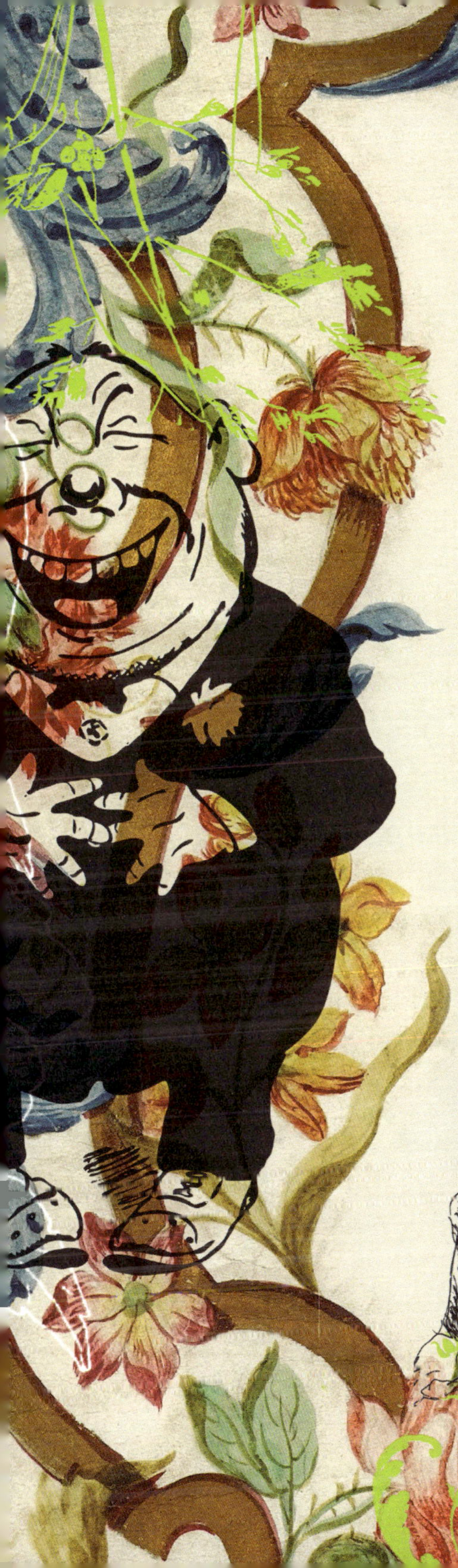

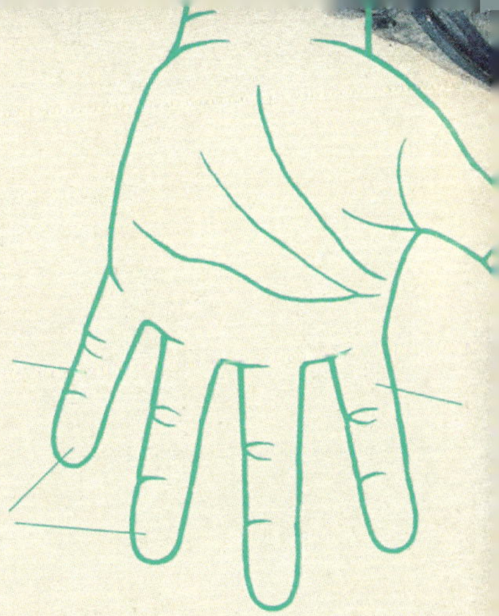

But even as they sat there looking glum, the big Toes doodling little circles on the sand were trying to figure out a challenge of their own. Finally, it was the turn of Legs. Their challenge, they said, was simple: Hands should carry the whole body from one part of a circle to the other.

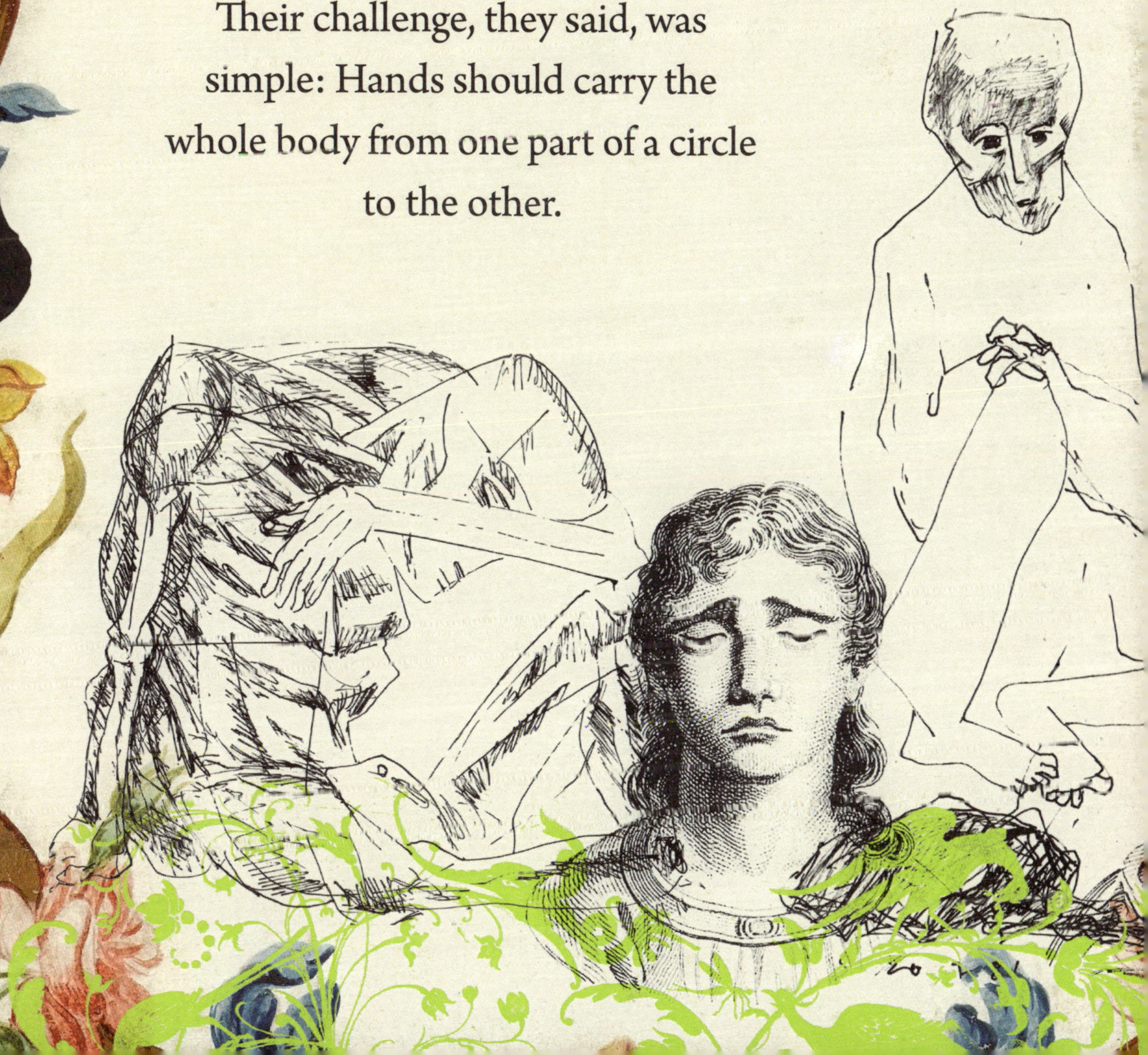

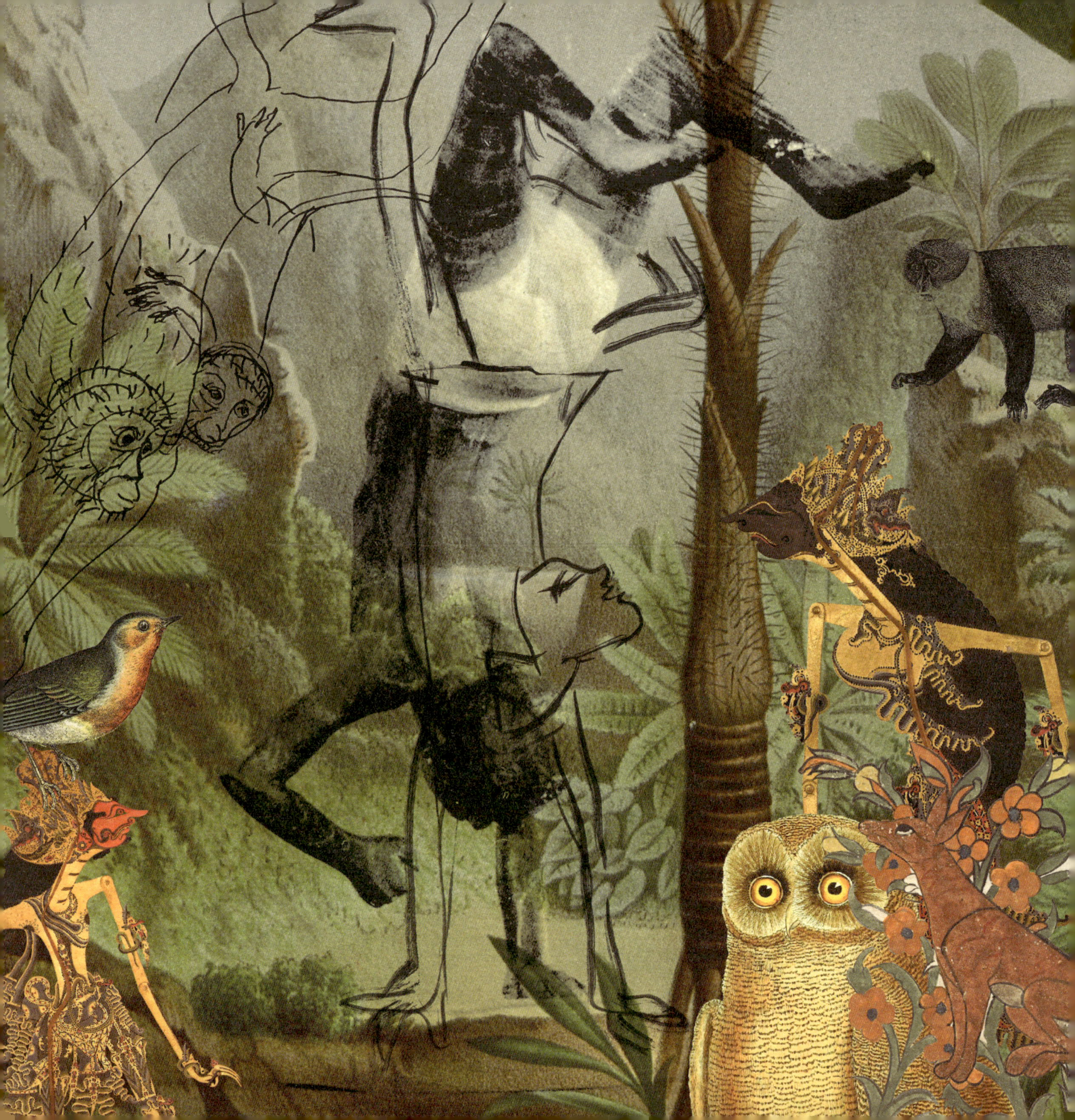

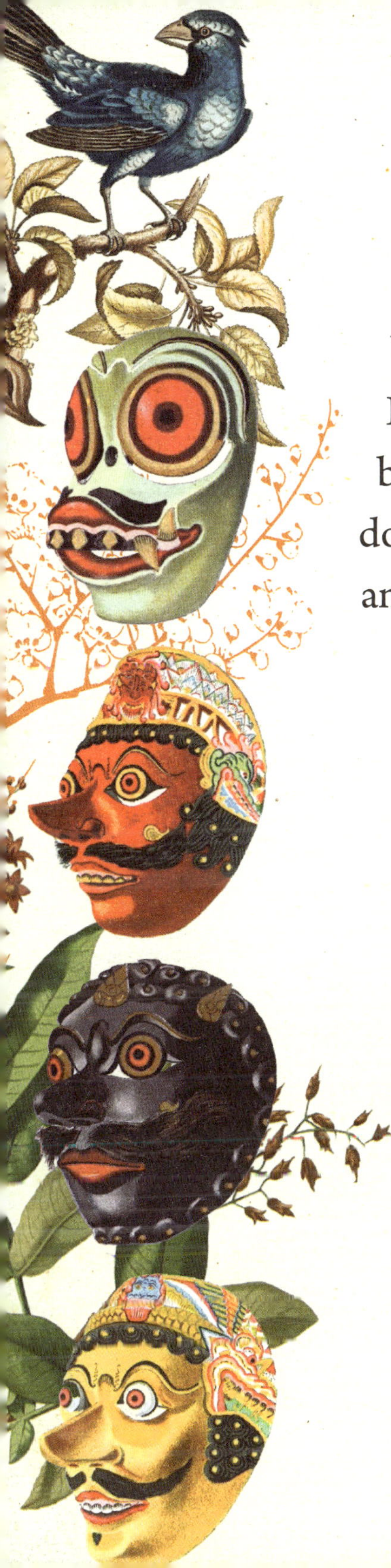

What a stupid challenge, thought arrogant Fingers. Yet it was a sight to see! The whole body was turned upside down! Hands came down and Legs went up; Eyes came down too, and could barely see anything but the ground; dust entered Nose, causing it to sneeze; and Toes wiggled in the air.

Nyayo juu, the spectators shouted, and then sang playfully.

Nyayo Nyayo juu
Hakuna matata
Fuata Nyayo
Hakuna matata
Turukeni angani

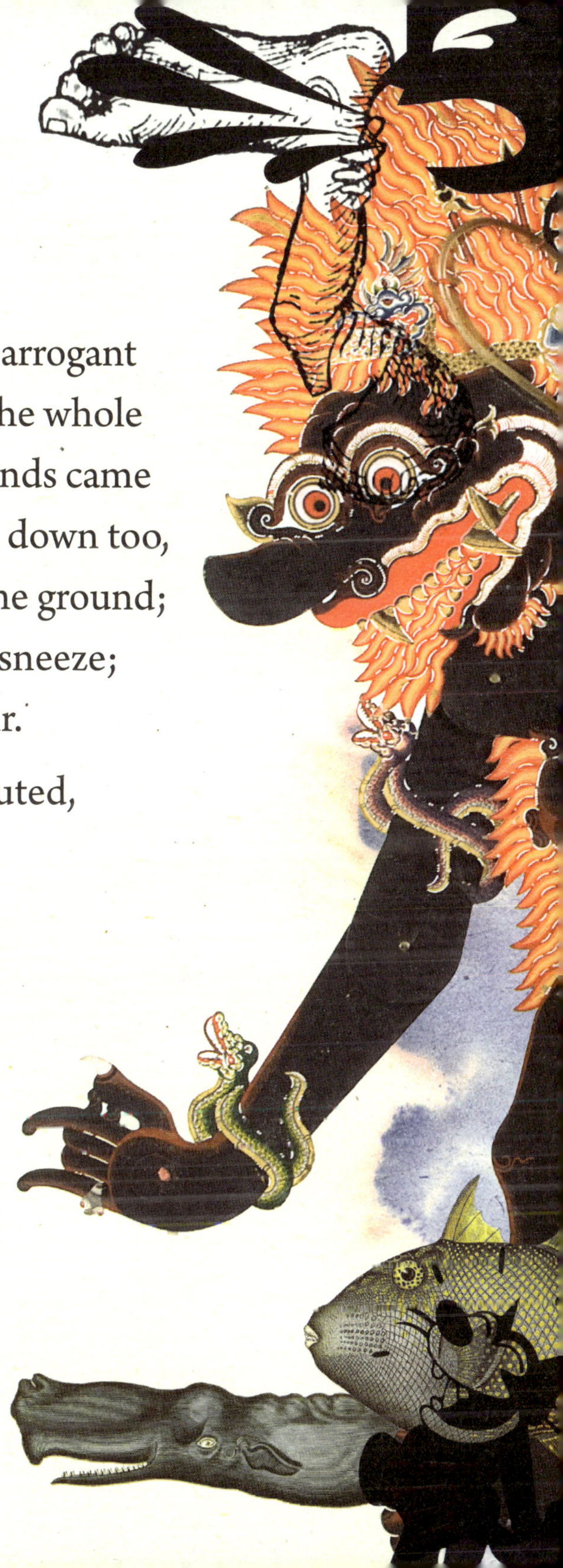

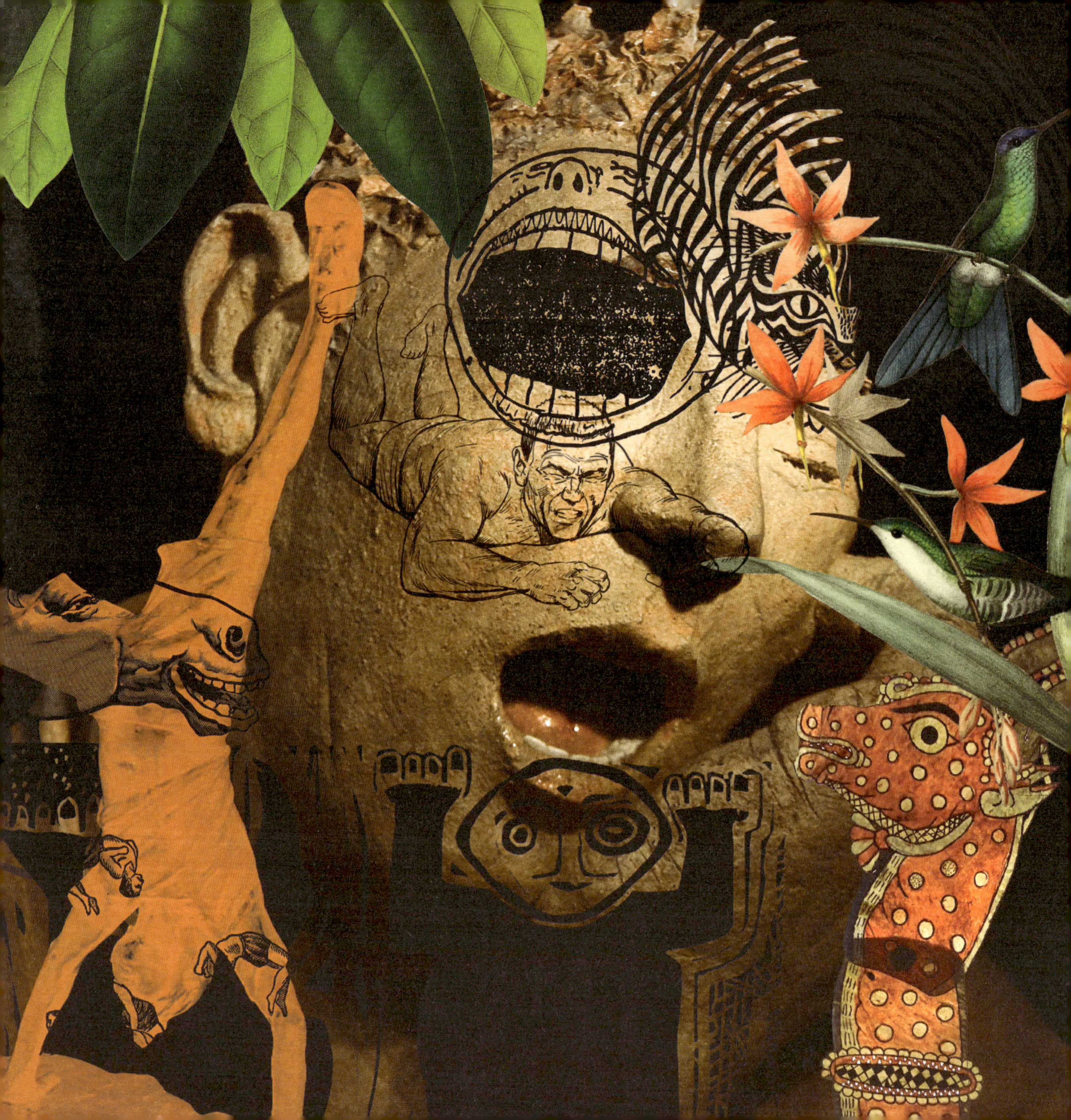

The eyes of the audience stayed fixed on Hands and Arms, who had displayed such an incredible array of skills—but now they could hardly move an inch. A few steps, and they cried out in pain and fell to the ground with a crash. They tried again, Fingers spreading out the better to hold the ground with but only Thumbs were able to stretch. They even tried cartwheels but that move was disqualified because it needed Legs.

Now it was the turn of Toes to laugh.

Hearing their scorn, Arms grew angry and made one last desperate attempt. But, alas, they could not move even a step.

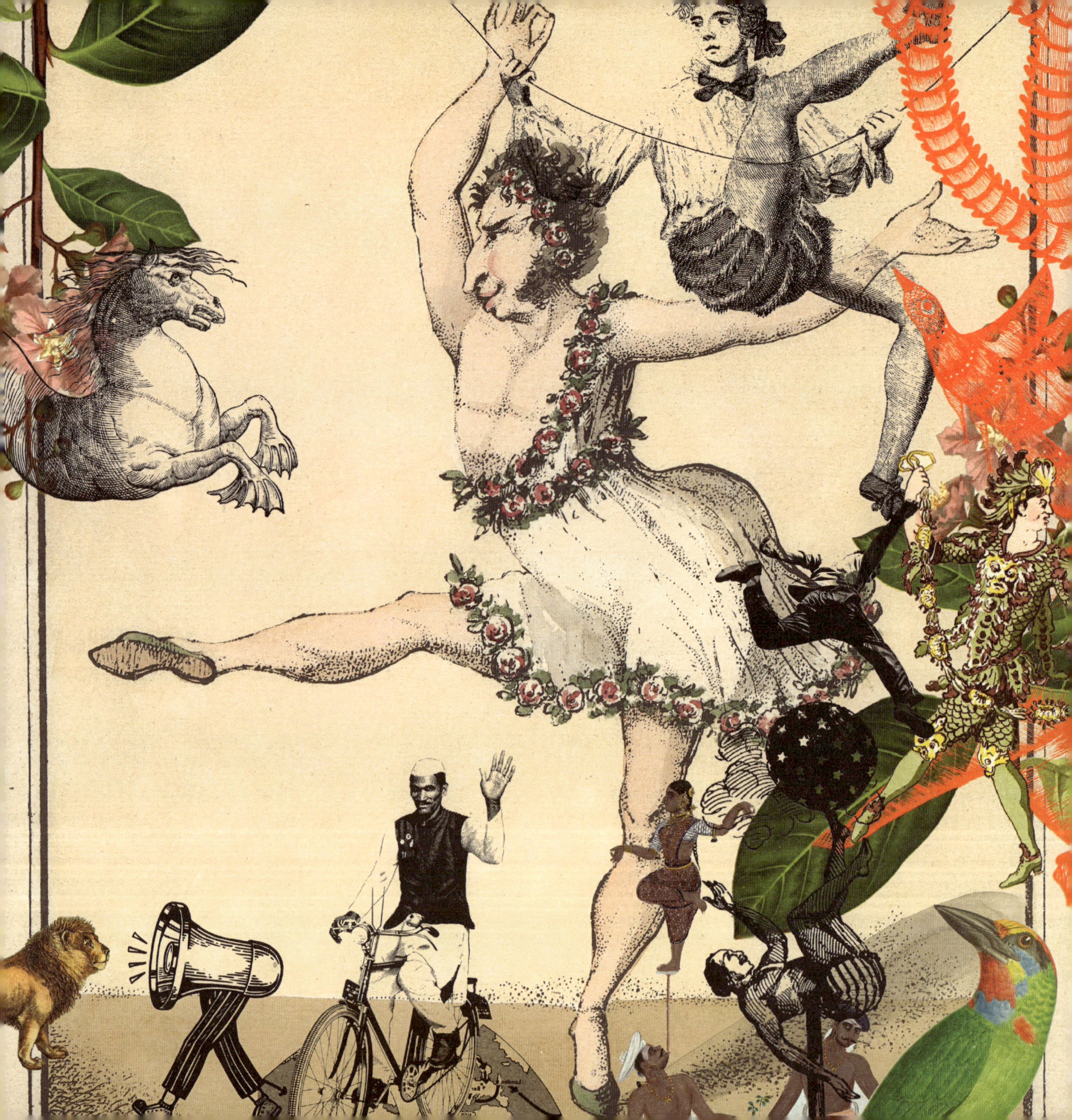

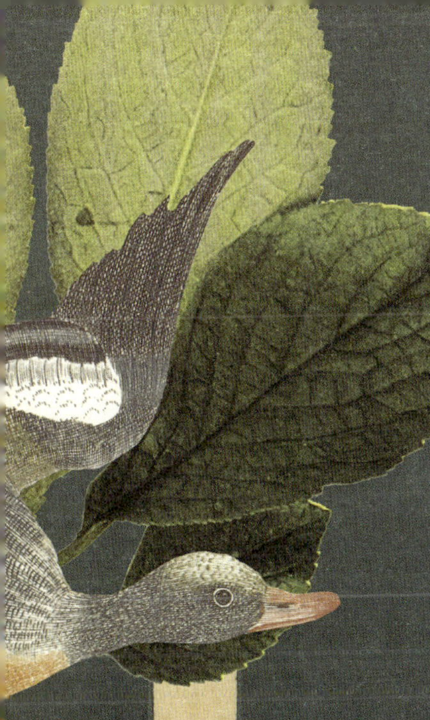

Exhausted, they gave up.

Now Legs began to show off what they could do—they marked time, they trotted, they ran, they made a few high jumps, even a few long jumps, without once letting the body fall.

The feet of the spectators stamped the ground in approval and solidarity.

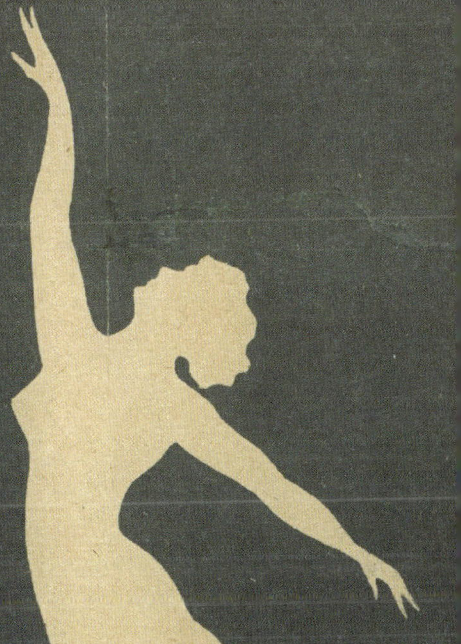

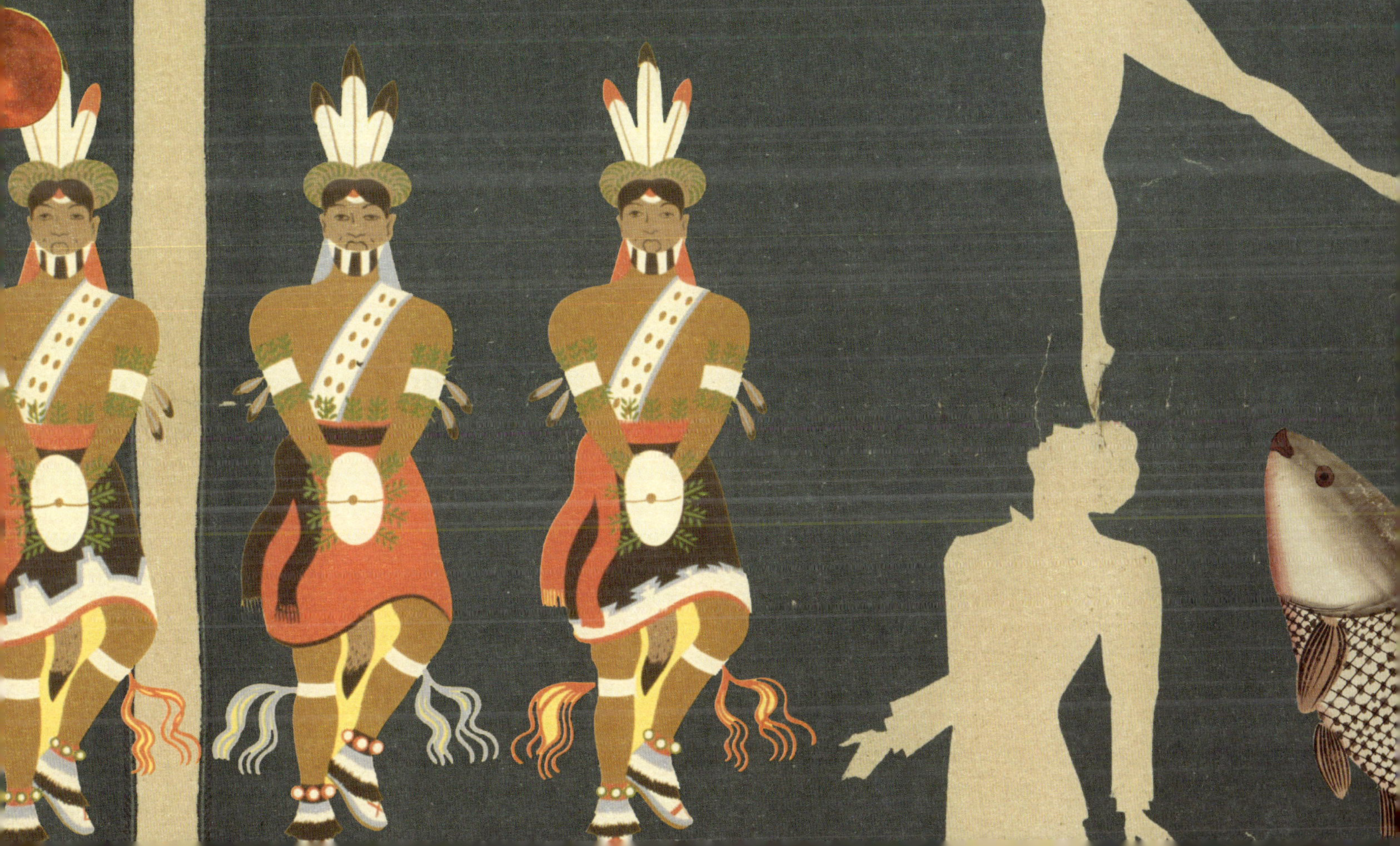

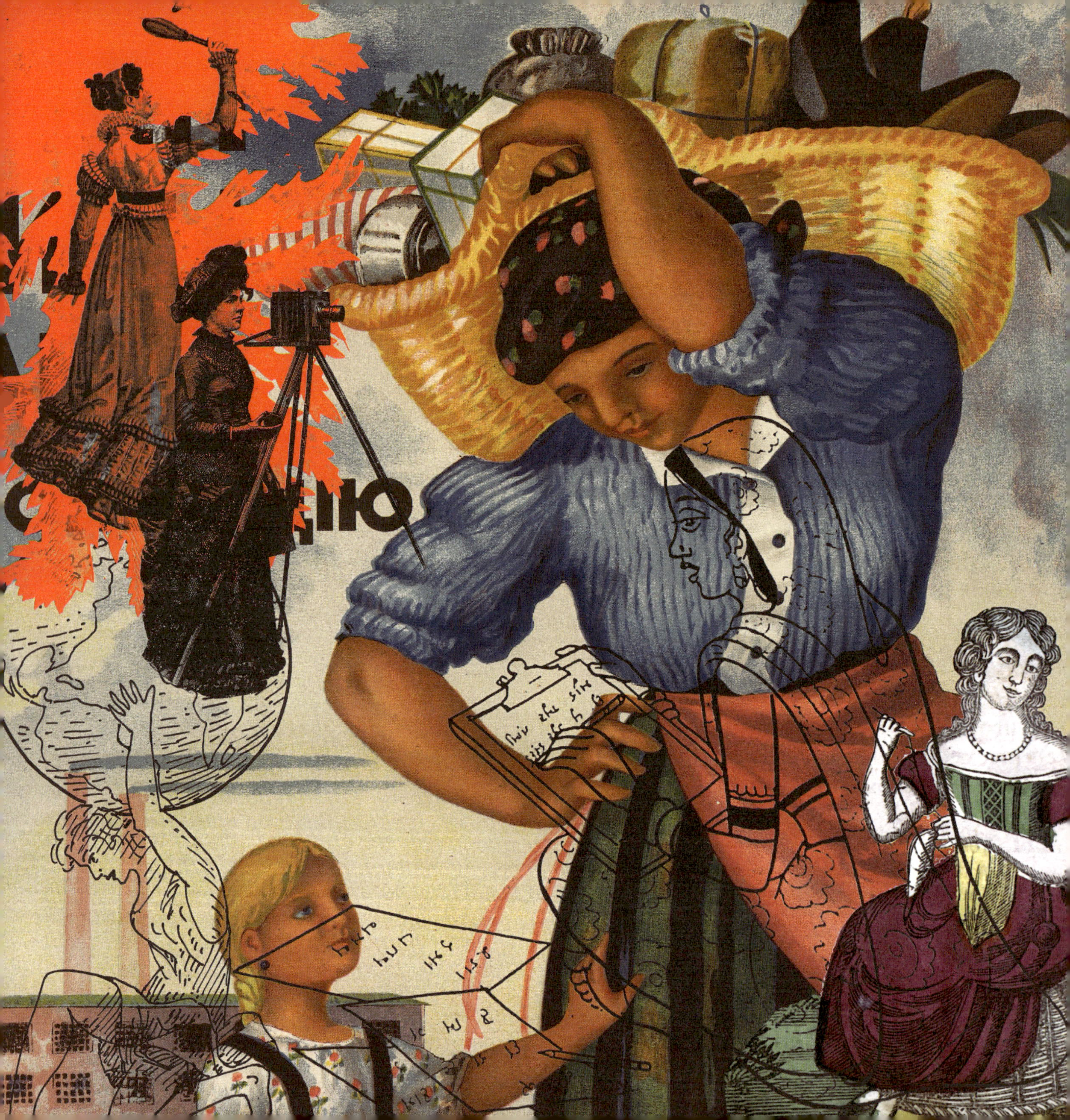

Suddenly everyone noticed something strange:
Thumbs, which had stretched out when
Hands were trying to carry the body,
remained separate from the other fingers.

Then they noticed that, far from making the
hands less efficient, it enhanced their clasping
and grasping, holding and unfolding power!

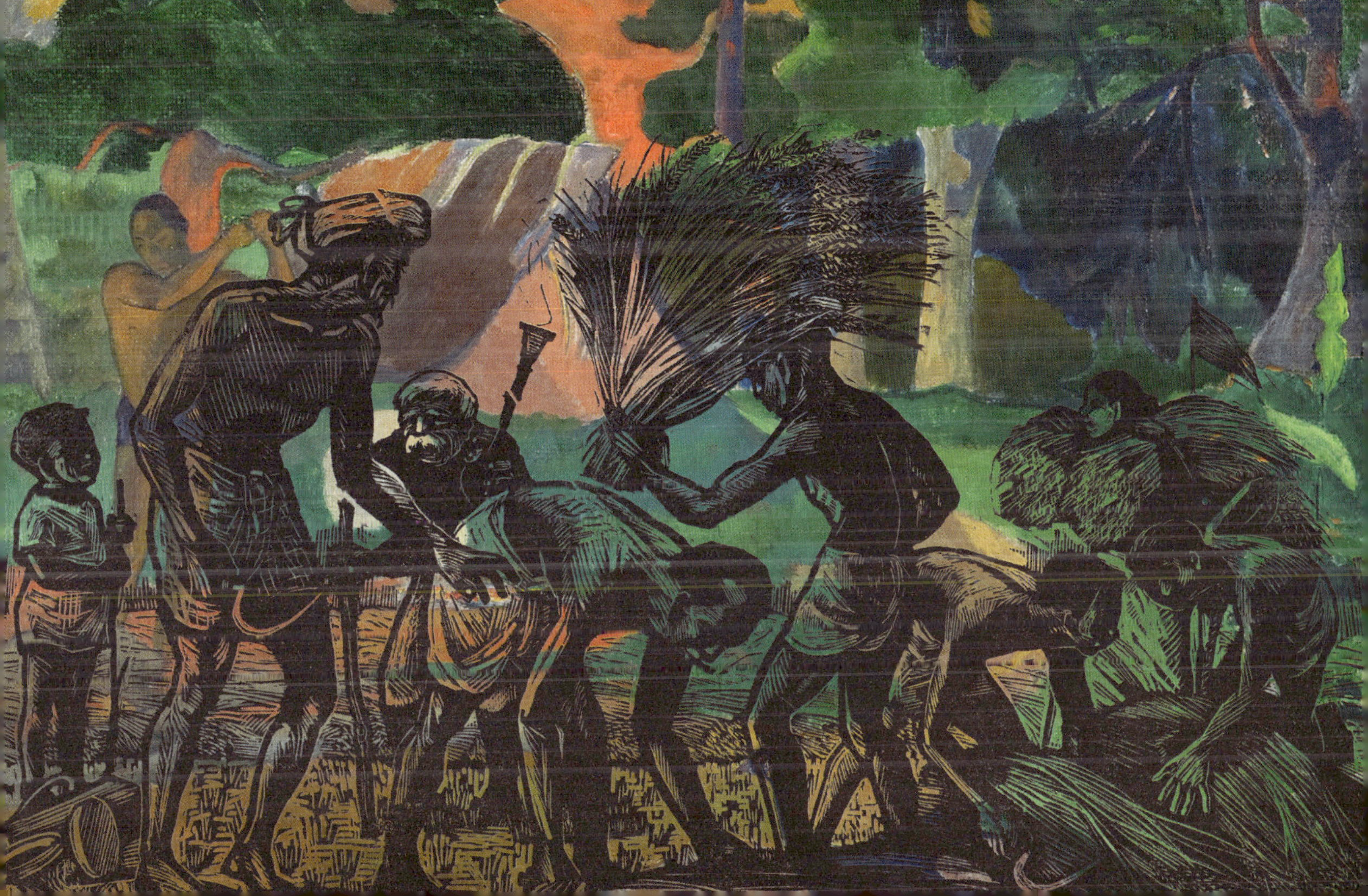

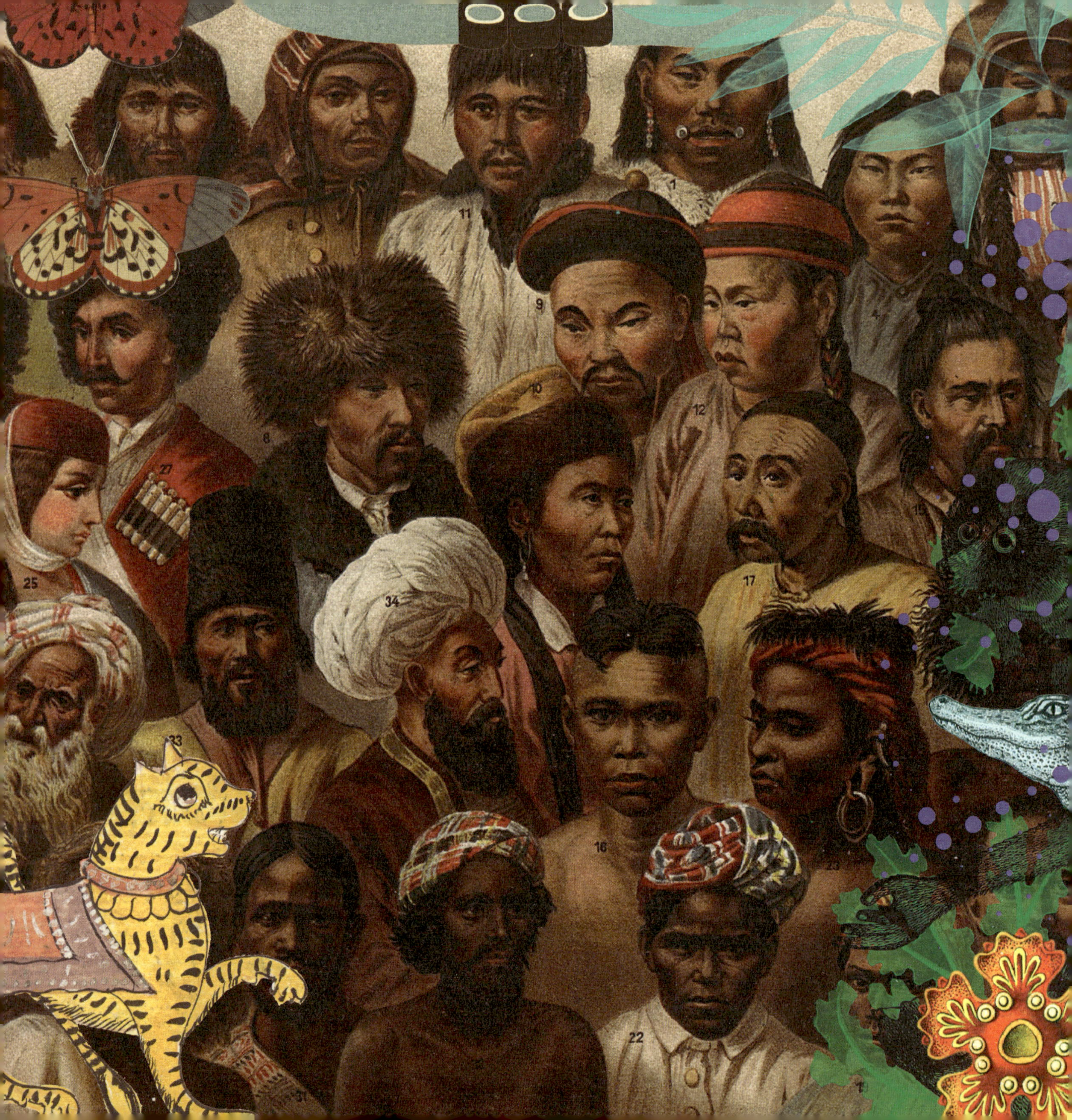

The debate among the organs went on for five days. But try as they could, they were not able to decide—each set of limbs was best at what it did, and none could do without the other.

What was the body anyway, they all wondered, and then realized—the body was *all of them together*!

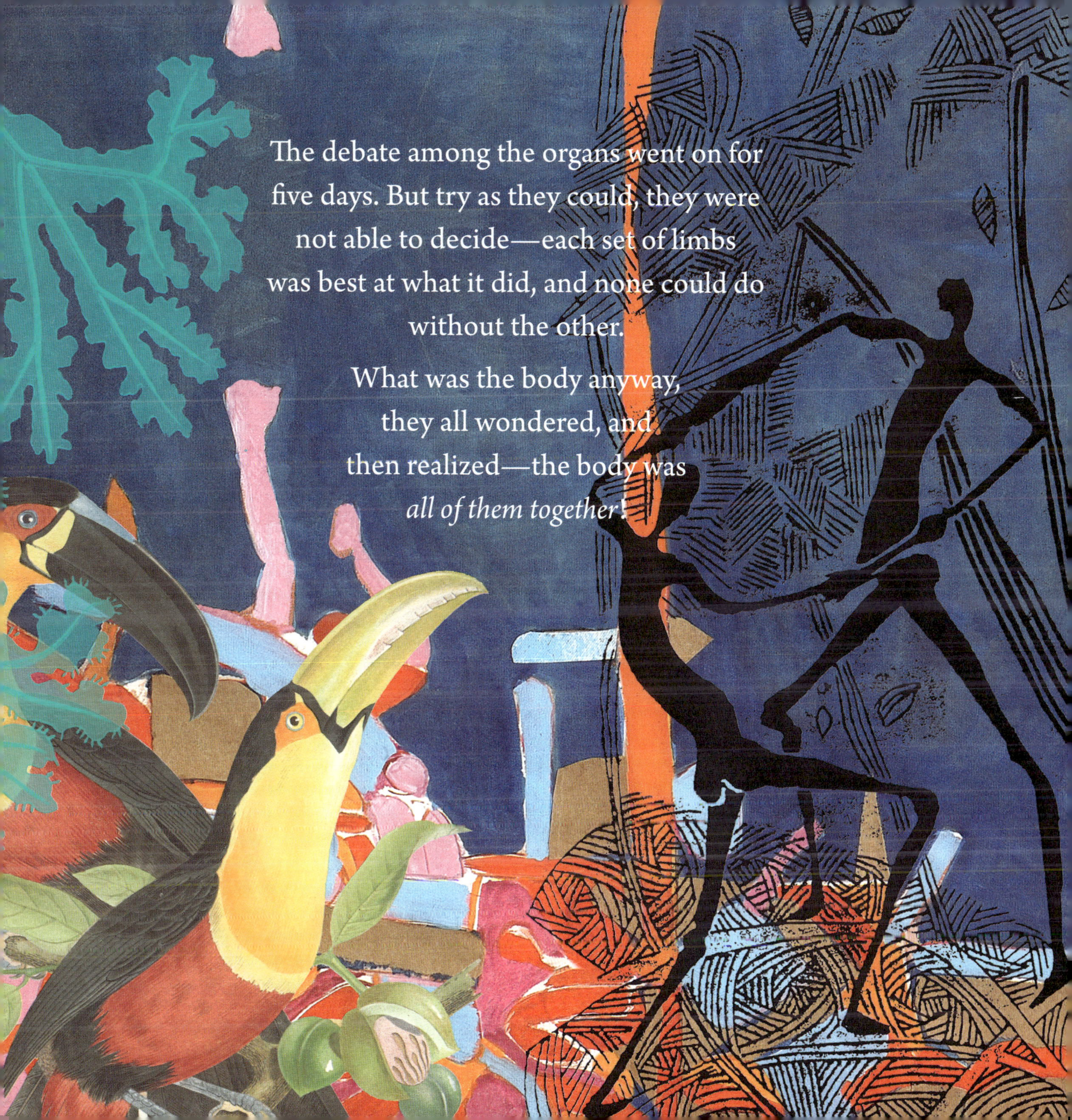

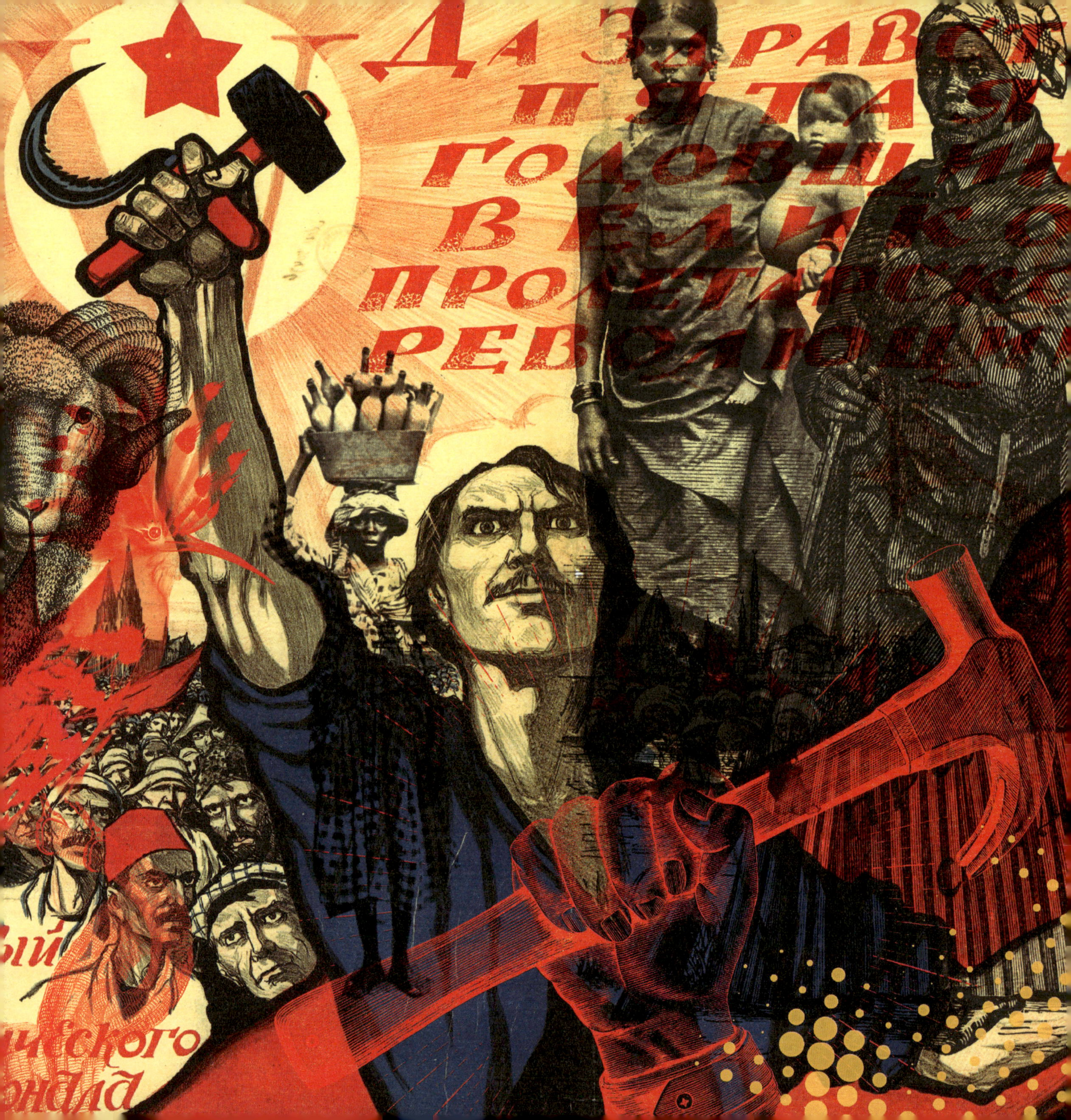

ДА З РАВ
ГОДОВЩ
ПРО ЕТАР
РЕВО
ЫЙ
ческого
онала

Henceforth, it was decided that
the body would stand upright—
Feet firmly planted on the ground,
Hands ready to work.
Only children would be allowed
to move on all fours for a while
so as not to forget their origins.

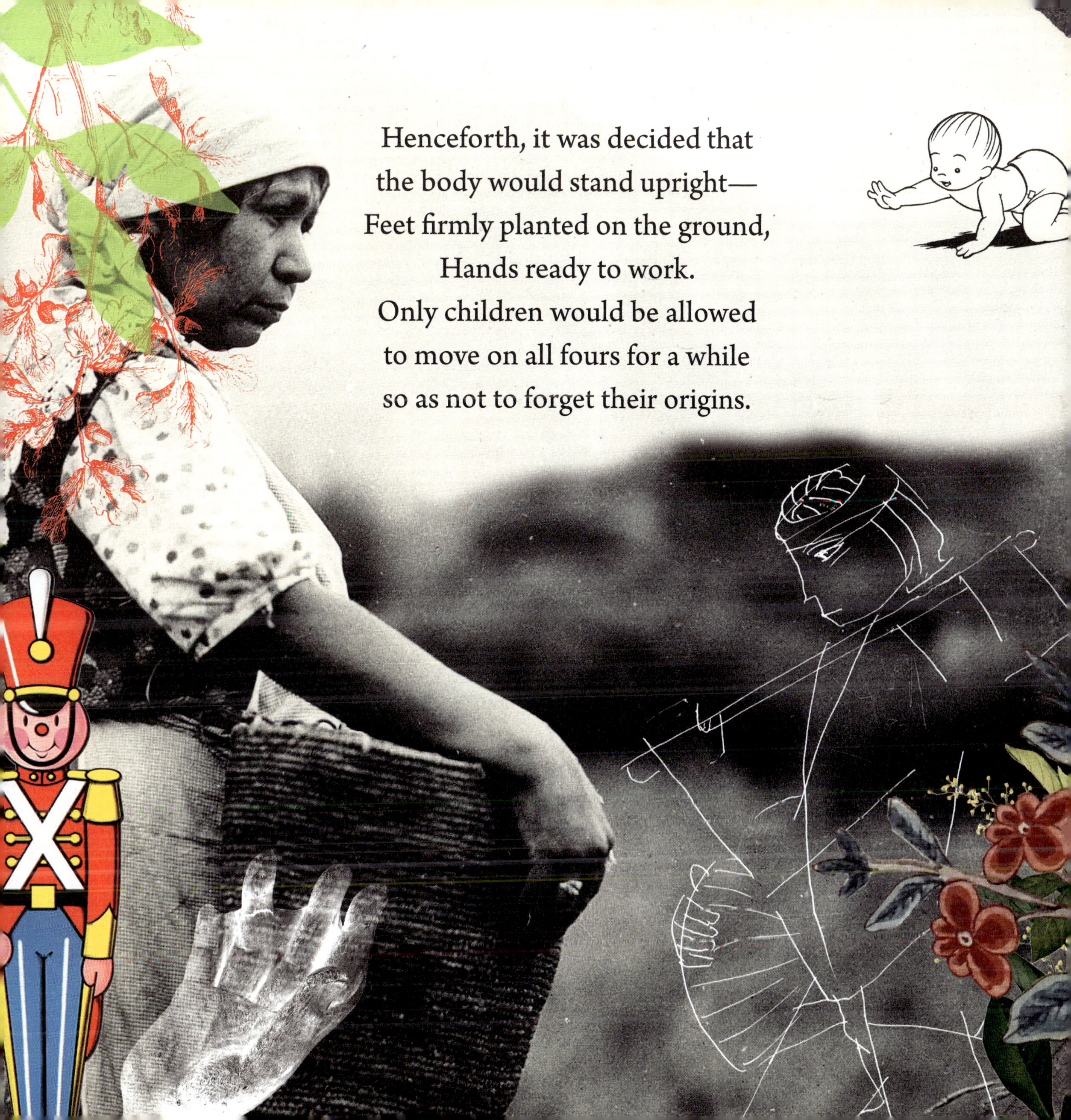

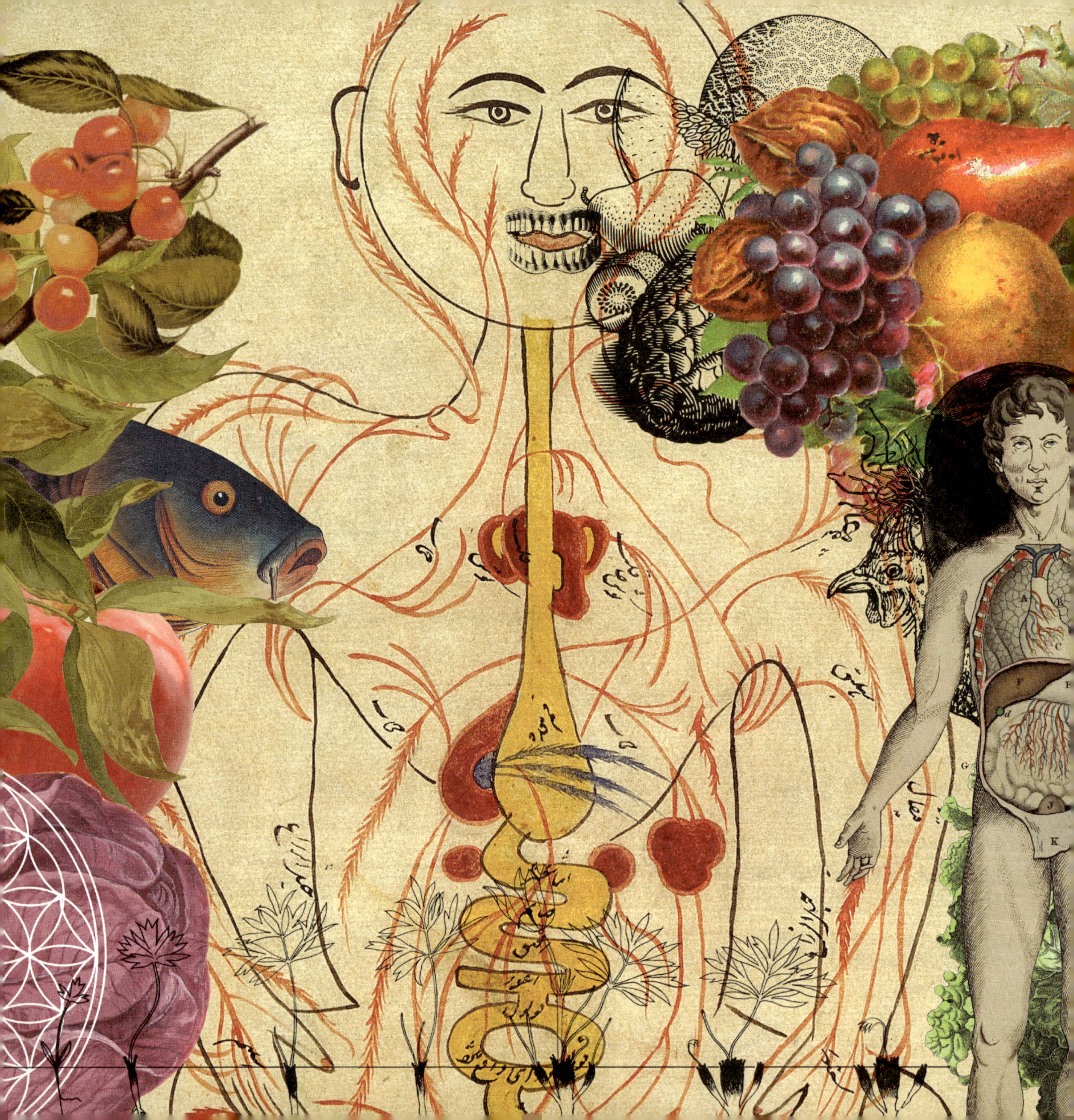

Legs and Feet would carry the body from place to place, and Arms and Hands would work with the environment, especially to put food into the mouth.

In the mouth, Teeth would chew the food and send it down the throat to the tummy. The tummy would squeeze all the goodness out of it, then pour it into its system of canals and send it to every nook and cranny.

Then the intestine would take the used materials and throw it out, bury it under the soil to enrich it. Plants would grow and bear fruit; the hands would pick some of it and put it in the mouth.

The circle of life.

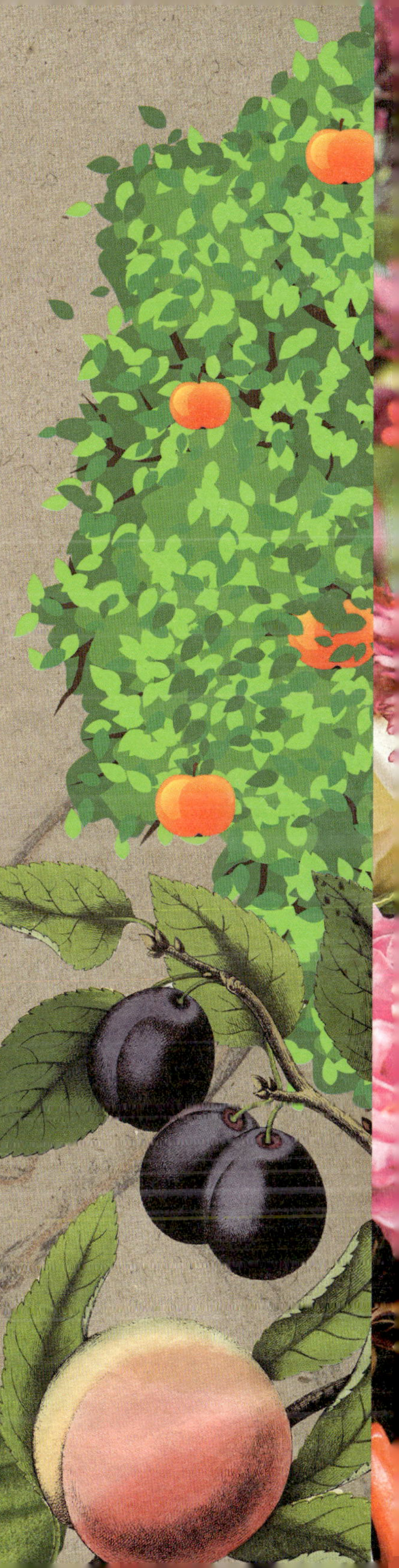

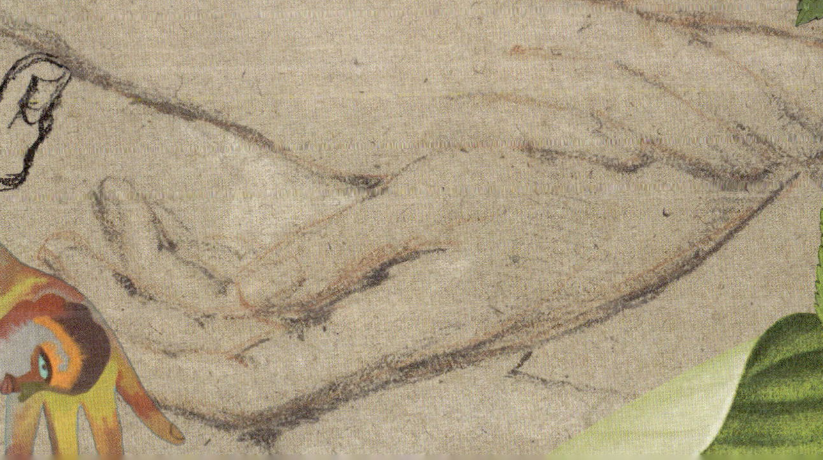

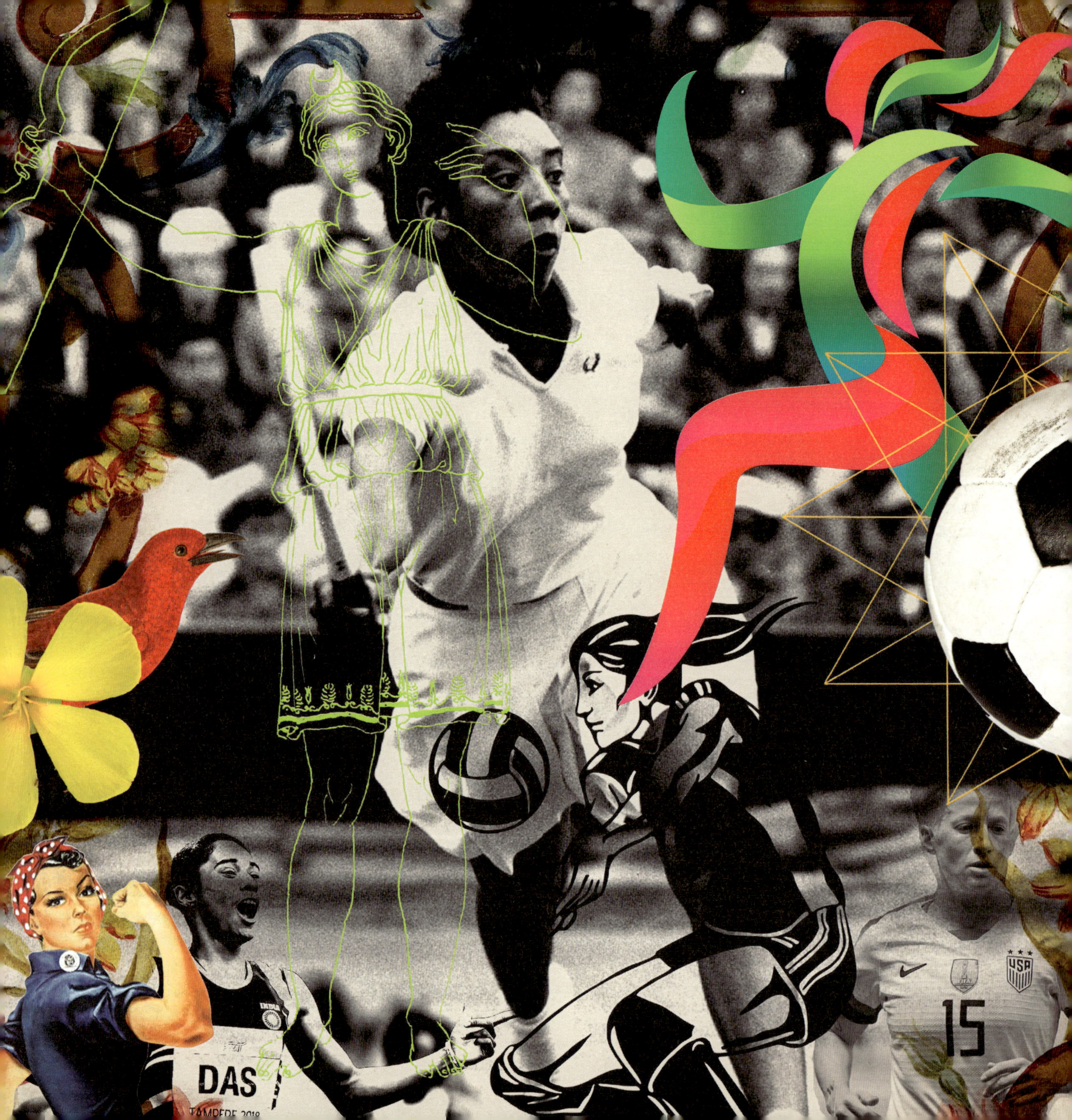
DAS
USA
15

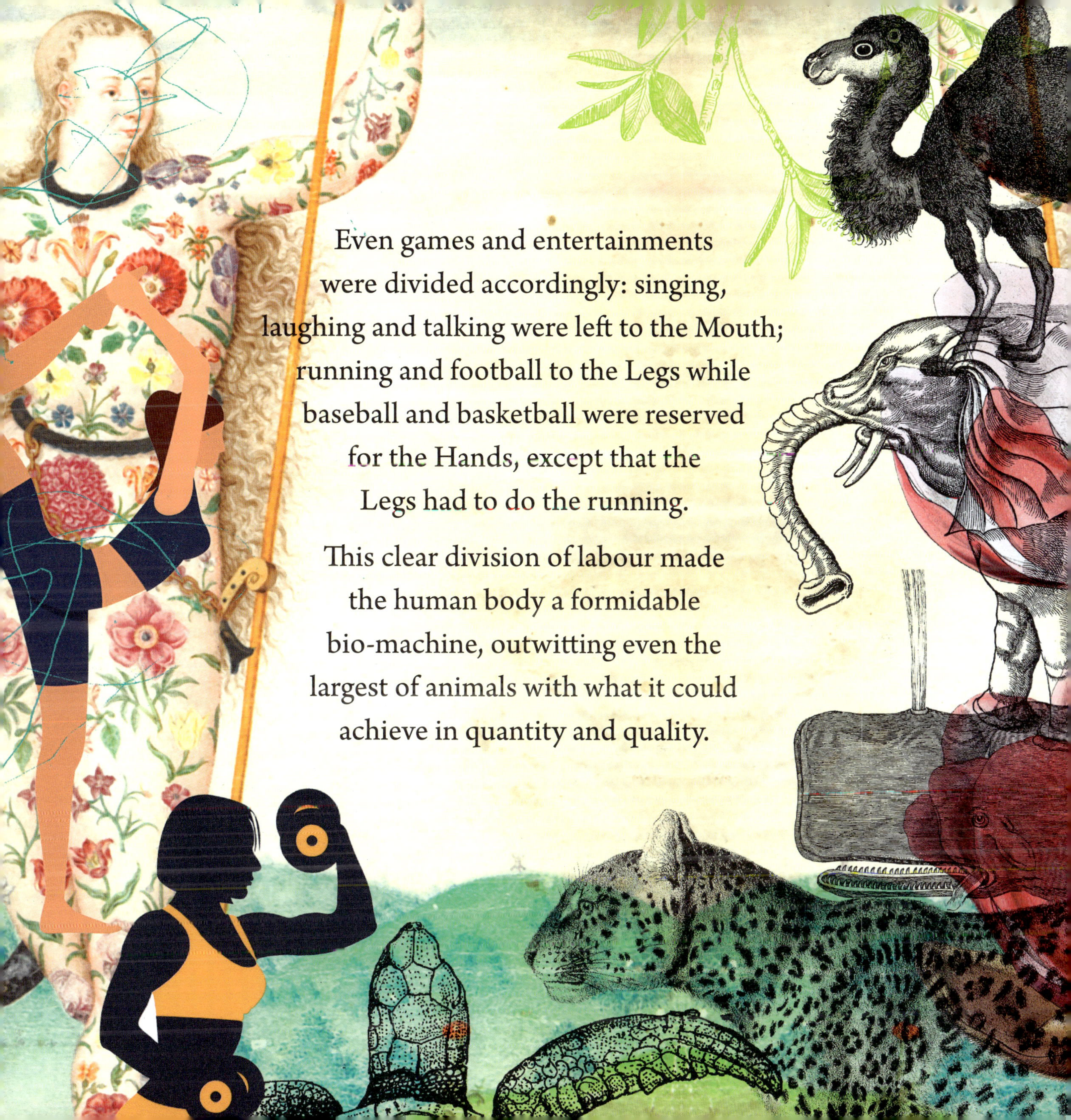

Even games and entertainments were divided accordingly: singing, laughing and talking were left to the Mouth; running and football to the Legs while baseball and basketball were reserved for the Hands, except that the Legs had to do the running.

This clear division of labour made the human body a formidable bio-machine, outwitting even the largest of animals with what it could achieve in quantity and quality.

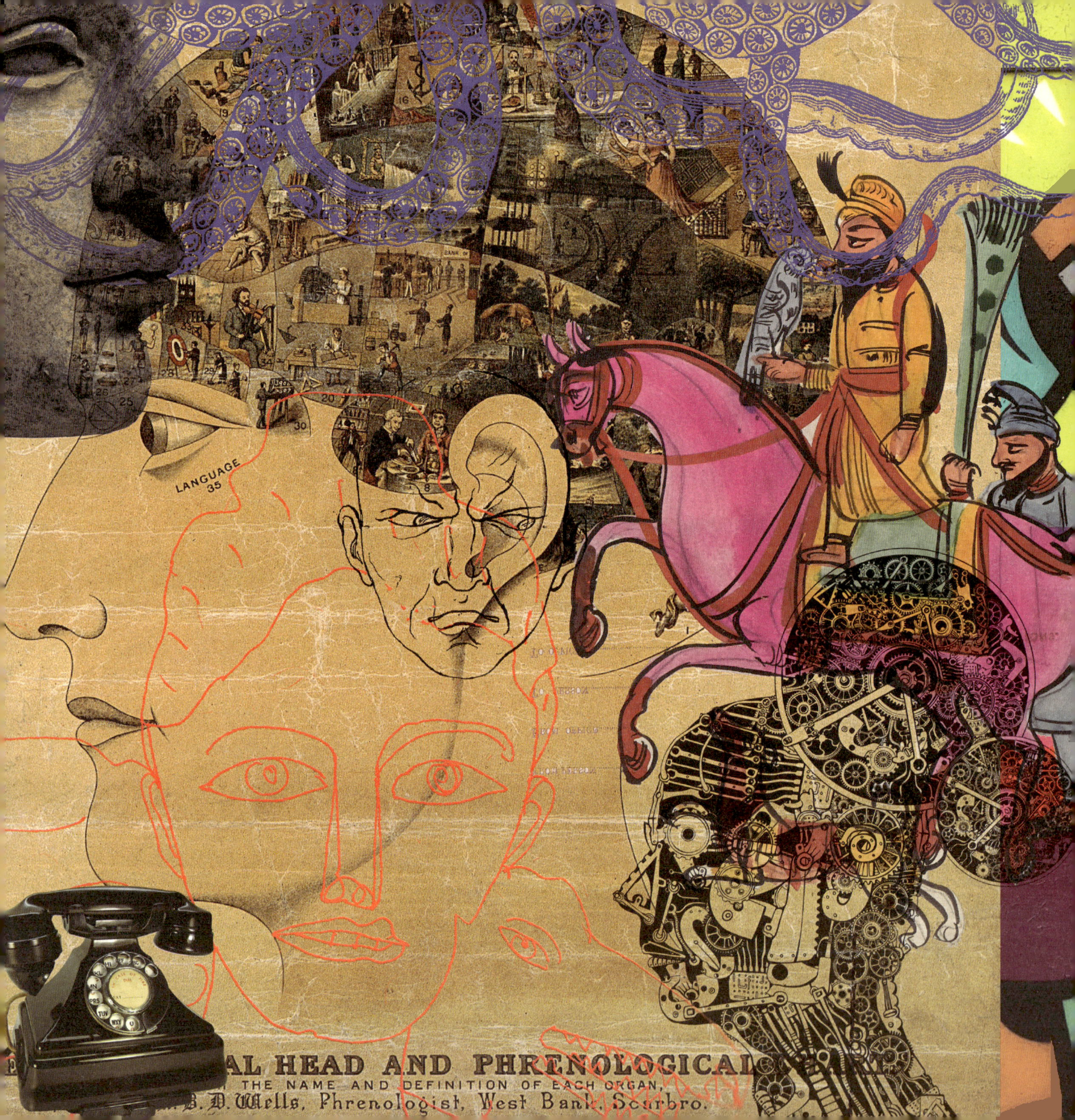

LANGUAGE
35
AL HEAD AND PHRENOLOGICAL
THE NAME AND DEFINITION OF EACH ORGAN,
B. D. Wells, Phrenologist, West Bank

However, the organs realized that this arrangement could still bring conflict—Head might feel it was the master of the organs below it.

But every part of the body was equal.

So the organs made sure that the pain and joy of any one was felt by all. And they warned the Mouth to remember that when it said 'my this' and 'my that', it was not speaking for itself but for *all* of them.

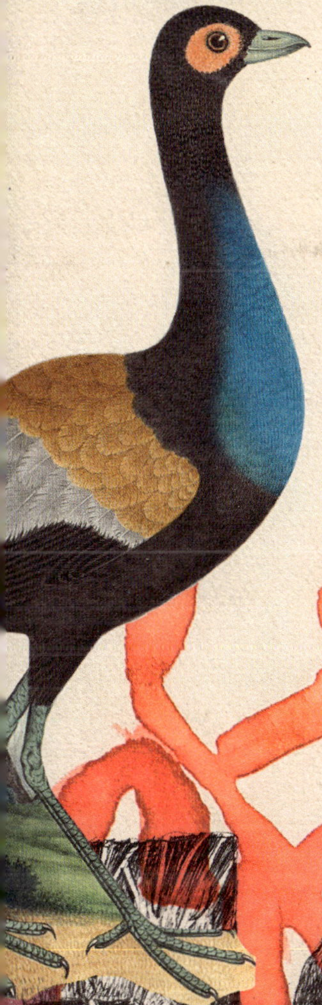

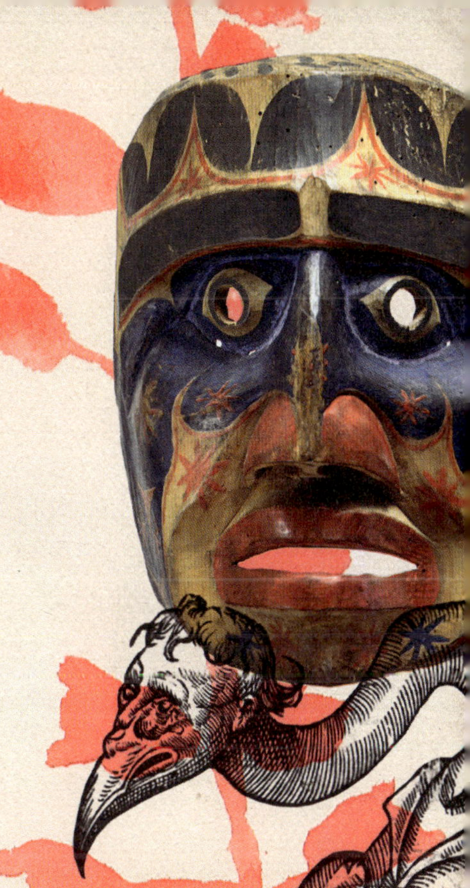

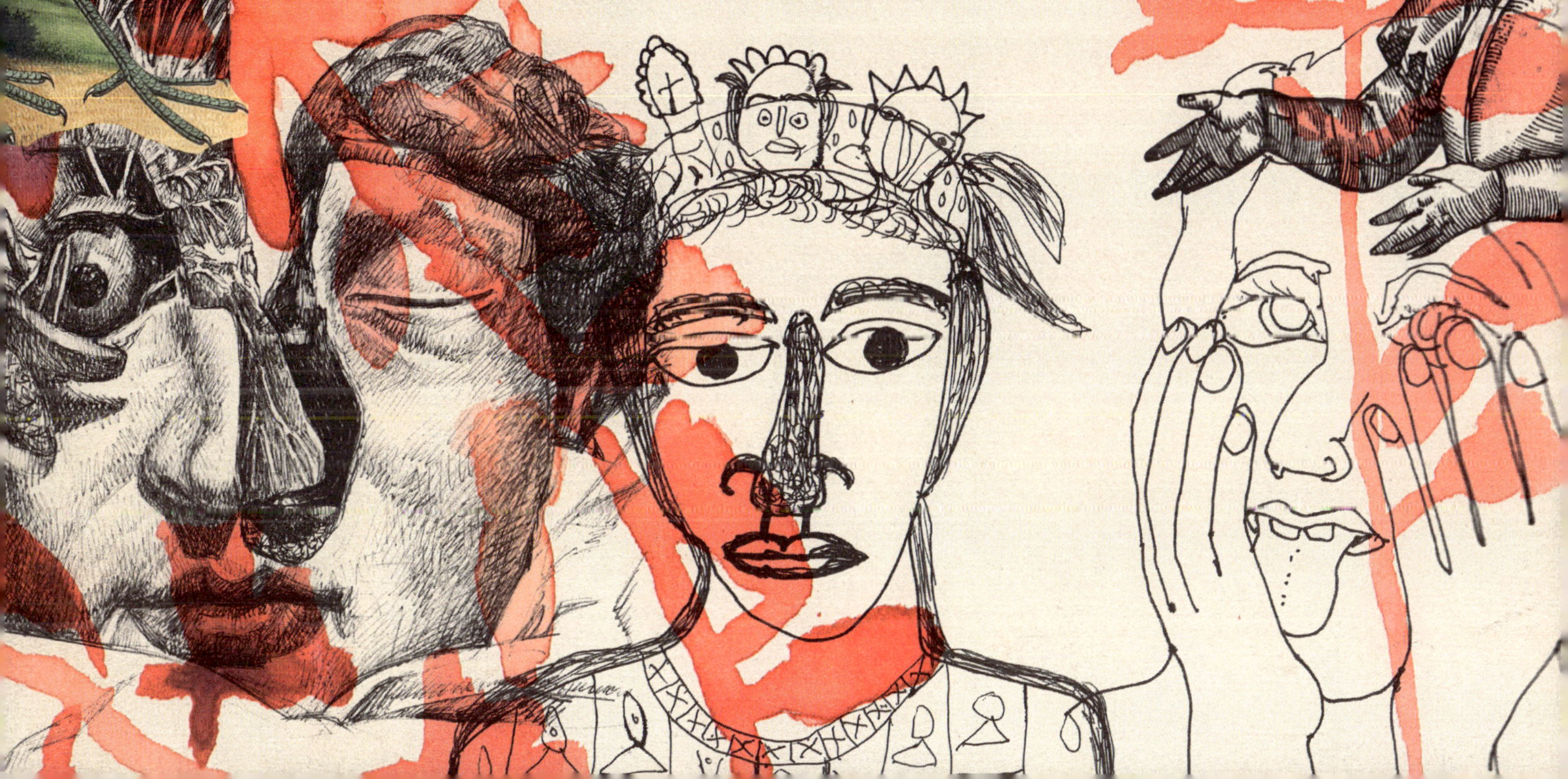

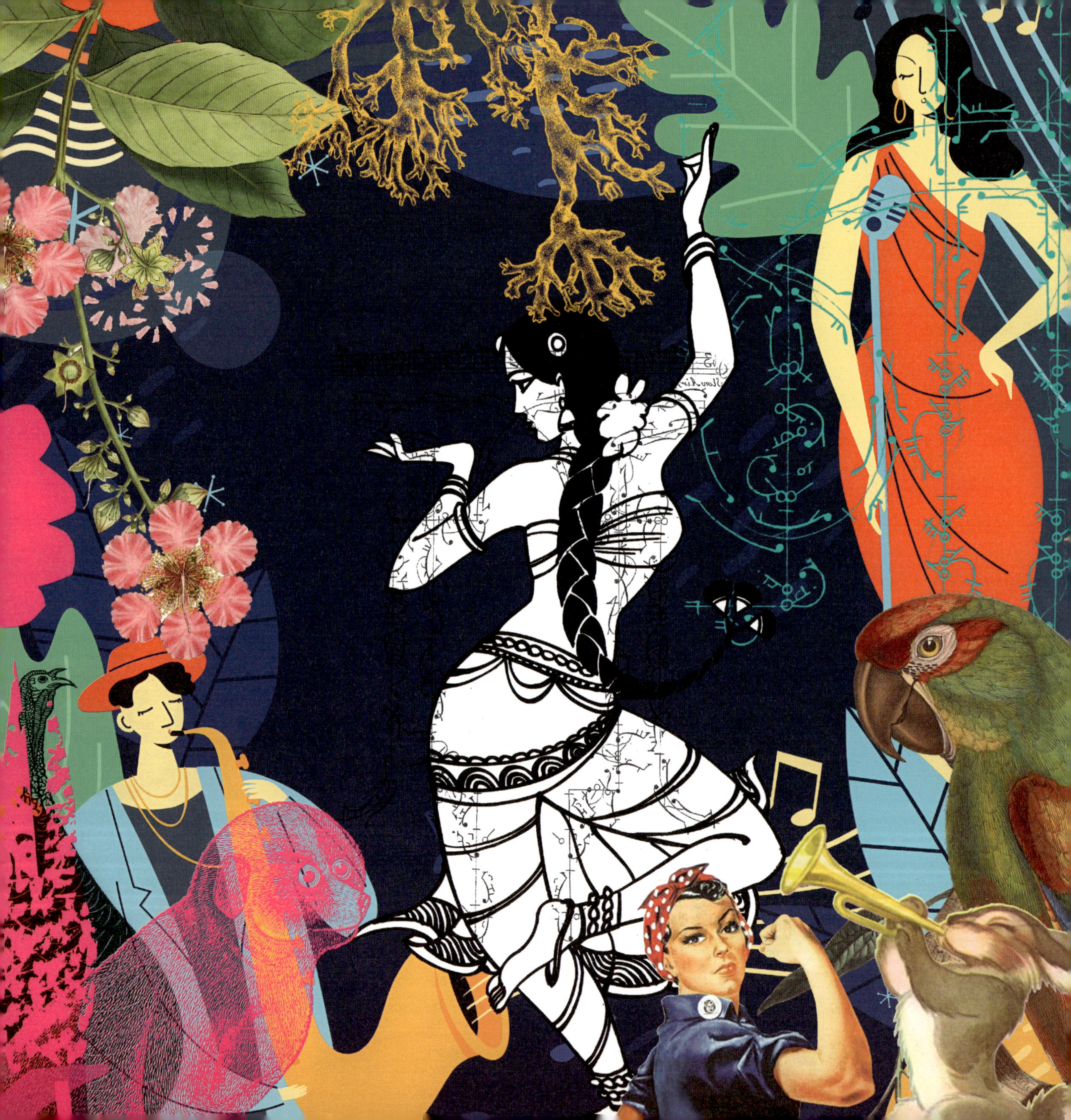

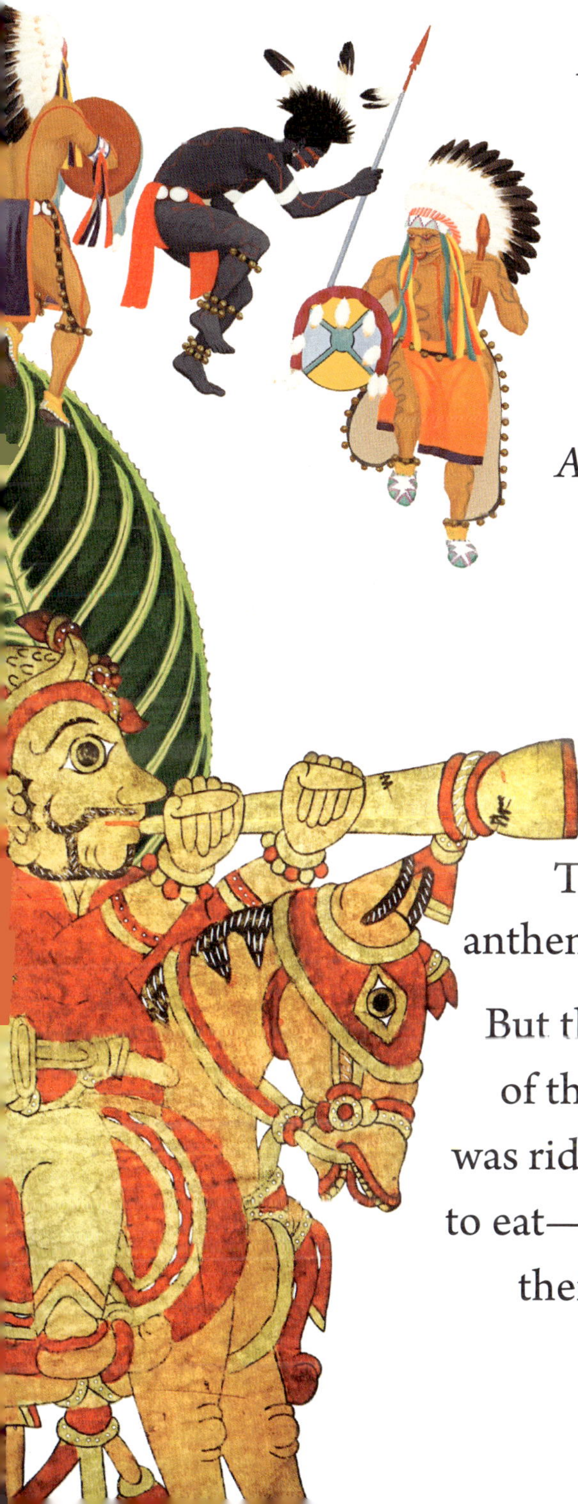

All together, they sang:

We are one body
There's no servant
We serve each other
The tongue is our voice
Hold me and I hold you
All together we are the body
All together we are one
Beauty is unity
Together we work
For a healthy body
Unity is our power

This became the All Body anthem, which they sing to this day.

But the animals would have none of this. All that singing business was ridiculous. The mouth was made to eat—and not to sing. They stuck to their ways, refusing to change their habits.

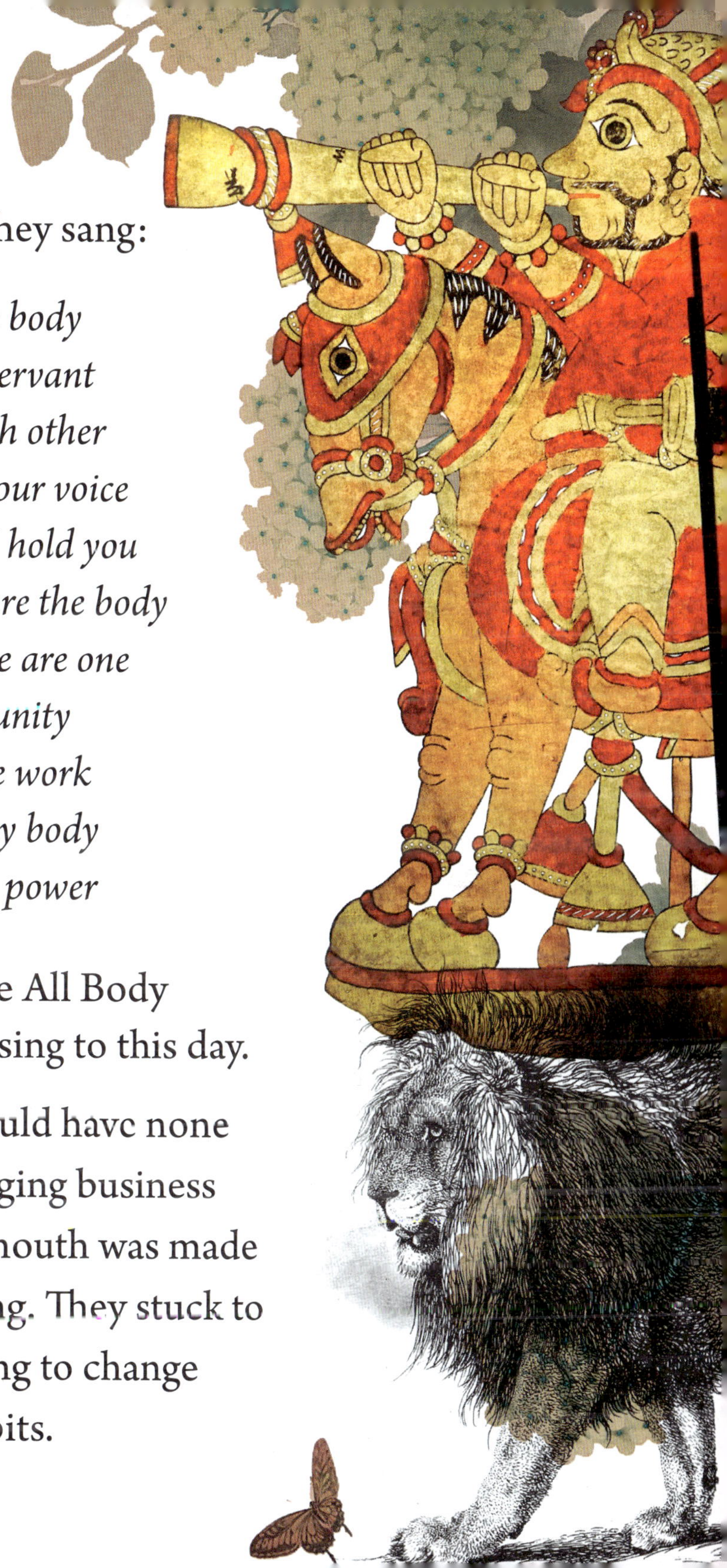

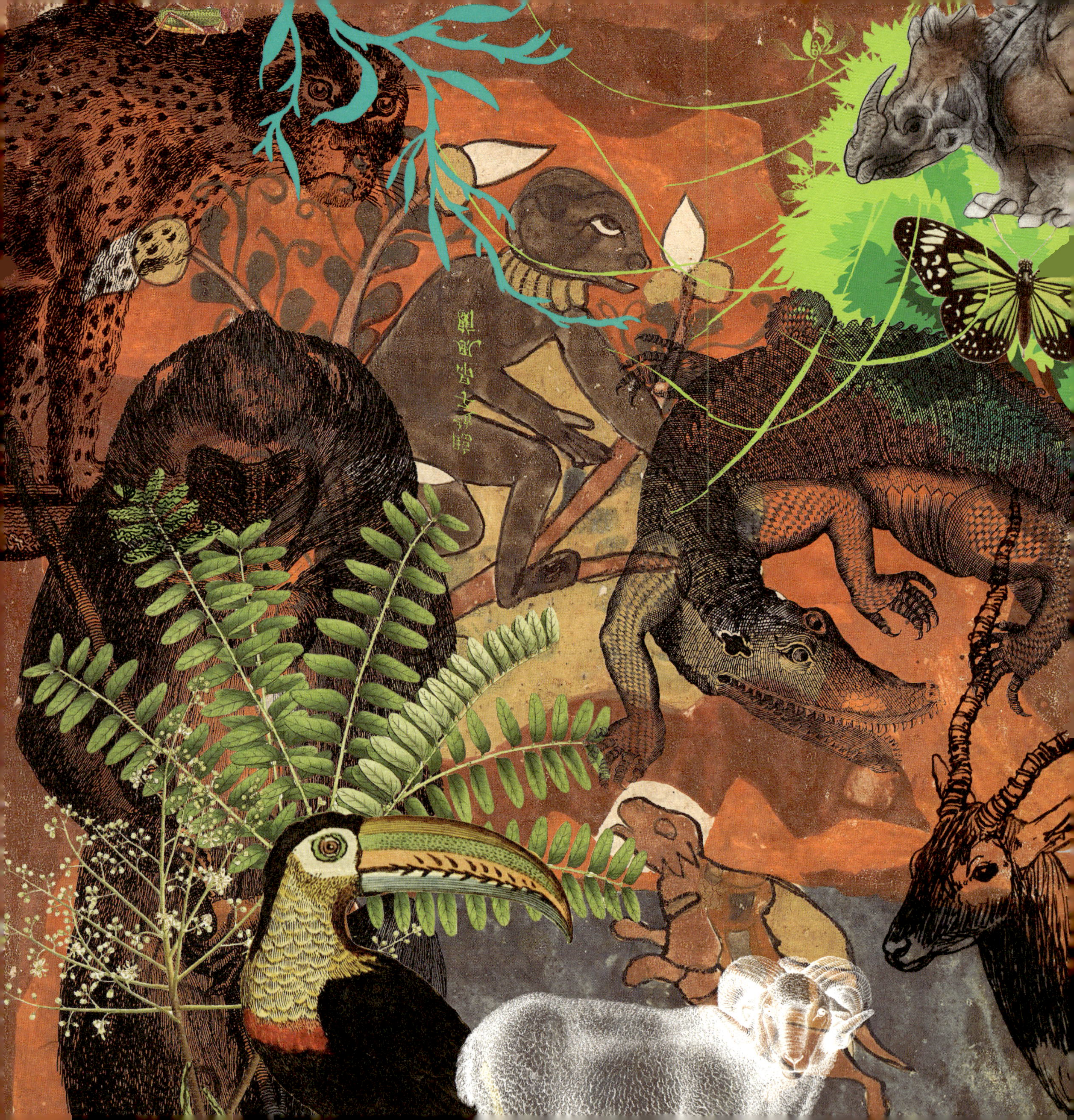

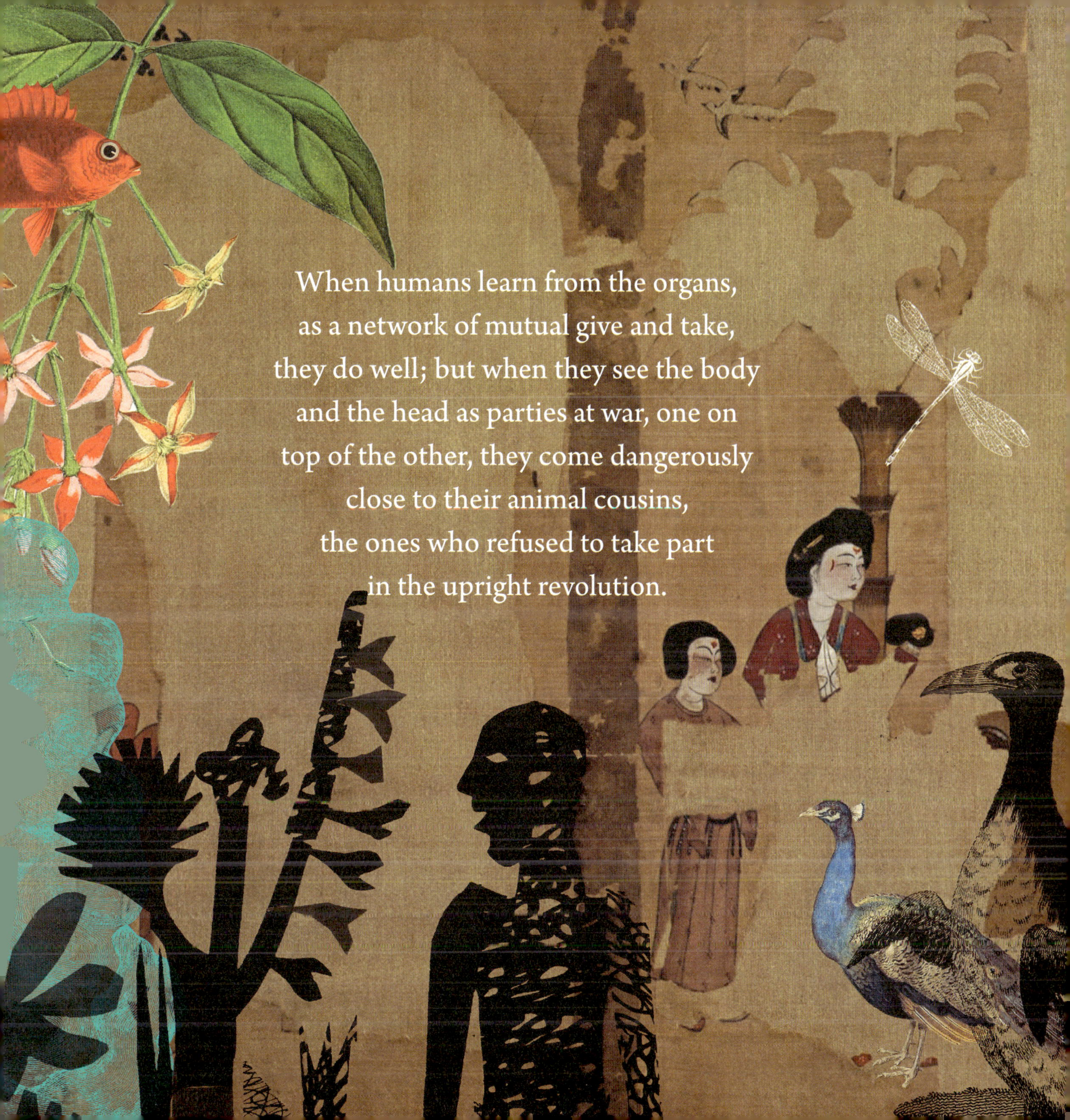

When humans learn from the organs,
as a network of mutual give and take,
they do well; but when they see the body
and the head as parties at war, one on
top of the other, they come dangerously
close to their animal cousins,
the ones who refused to take part
in the upright revolution.

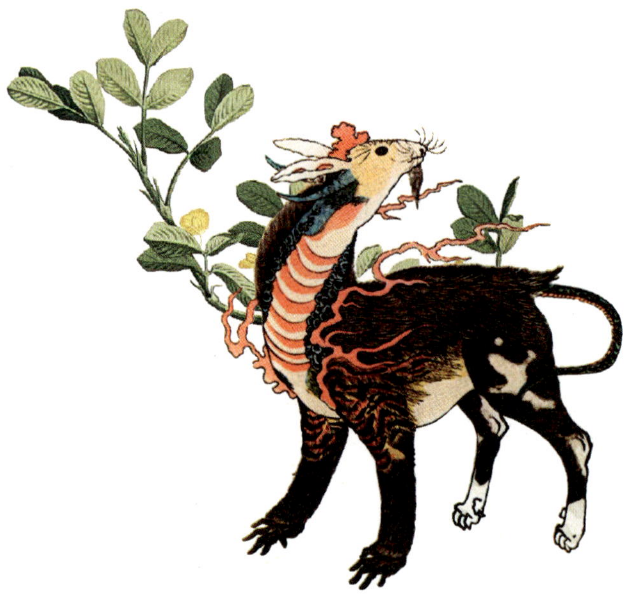